Angel
Manifesto

ANGEL MANIFESTO

MICHAEL FOOT

Matador
9 Priory Business Park,
Wistow Road, Kibworth Beauchamp,
Leicestershire. LE8 0RX
Tel: 0116 279 2299
Email: books@troubador.co.uk
Web: www.troubador.co.uk/matador
Twitter: @matadorbooks

ISBN 978 1789016 338

British Library Cataloguing in Publication Data.
A catalogue record for this book is available from the British Library.

Printed and bound in Great Britain by 4edge Limited
Typeset in 11pt Aldine401 BT by Troubador Publishing Ltd, Leicester, UK

Matador is an imprint of Troubador Publishing Ltd

This book is dedicated to Gene Ludwig, a very good friend on whose innate optimisn about life I drew whenever I hit a roadblock in writing this book.

My thanks go to Canon Robert Wright. He created the cover of this book. You can see examples of his increasingly well-known abstract paintings on robertwrightartist.co.uk. He also kindly confirmed that I was not taking undue liberties with my excursion in the book into the theology of angels.

I am also very grateful to Nicola and her colleagues in the Buckland Book Club. They persuaded me to tie up some important elements in the story and add 2 sections towards the end of the book.

1

Andrew Davies stepped quietly and unobtrusively into the street. It housed his bank's HQ in the City of London, various coffee shops and fast food outlets, and a few offices for smaller firms. It was 5.30 p.m., and already the street was crowded with people using it as a short cut up to Liverpool Street for the evening commute. The bank's exit was set back a little from the road and Andrew paused there a minute before heading against the main flow, towards Moorgate.

It was a fairly early end of the day for him but he had been at his desk from just after 7 a.m.; and there were still members of his team monitoring the IT filters and dealing with the remaining 'red flags' from that day's work. The New York office, of course, had been up and running for hours too; but in his bank it was the accepted rule that London sorted out the problems that had been generated in Europe; and so London staff could –if they wished and often if they did not wish – work into late evening.

Normally, the end of his working day meant a 14 minute stroll back to the apartment he rented, down towards Tower Hill. (He would have called it a 'flat' when he was young but now understood that, to pander to the residents' need for self-respect and sustain the price, it was an 'apartment'.) The City's decade of success (well, at least up to the screw-up of 2008 known more generally to the world as the Global Financial Crisis) had meant a growing number of refurbishments and new buildings like this one. Here he rented one of 109 apartments designed for professionals like him. They weren't cheap to own or, as in his case, rent. But they were close to most of the evening activities necessary for the young City executive and they each came with an internal basement parking space. Most importantly for him, there was no catching the last train out of town or trying to find a cab at 2 a.m. to take him south of the river. So he was very happy with what he had.

But tonight he was heading up to the Foreign & Commonwealth Office (FCO) in Whitehall. The chance of any of his work colleagues being around there and spotting his eventual entry, about 6.15, were almost zero; and, anyway, his cover story – for those work colleagues who did know something about his supposed background – provided a perfectly good excuse. The security at the gate took some convincing that he genuinely had an appointment outside normal office hours. When he was finally admitted, there was no Receptionist to show him into the Visitor's Waiting Room. He would have to await the arrival of the secretary of the man he knew as 'the Colonel' to collect him.

A slightly harassed and frumpy middle-aged woman came for him a few minutes later. Andrew had not met her before – indeed, he had only met the Colonel three times that he could recall. She wore what he thought were probably regulation clothes for secretaries at the FCO – ensuring that no personal feature good or bad should be particularly visible. In this spirit, she wore a shapeless long dress, topped with a woollen grey cardigan that had obviously seen many years' service. In his own organization, he was used to secretaries with an average age of 25; and who highlighted any good feature they had, by dressing in as little as possible and/ or in something tight. He could see there were some advantages to the FCO approach, especially as – unlike his own 'secretary' – he guessed this one could probably actually write and spell like an adult.

She appeared through the door and, without raising her eyes to his for a second, held out her hand saying *"I'm Sue, Mr. Mortby's secretary. It's very good of you to come so late. But Mr. Mortby spends so much of his time during the day in meetings; and, of course, we didn't want to interrupt your work by asking you to come over during the day. Anyway, please follow me."*

Andrew tried a little light conversation to make her relax (you never knew when a friendly secretary might be a useful asset) as they made their way to the Colonel's office. The façade of the building was impressive, but as you went deeper into its recesses the effect became more of an elderly country house whose owners had seen better times. As they waited for a lift that looked as though it had been one of the first ever installed, he glanced out of the window and saw major excavation works all neatly sealed off and mournfully quiet at this time of night. *"Having something major done there, are they?"* he asked. For the first time she actually glanced at his face; *"Oh no. They were digging to put in a small new security cabin and they found the base of a structure that was built for the Queen's Jubilee – Victoria's of course not Elizabeth's. Now they're trying to work out what to do with the ruins; and the environment lot won't let us just tear them out."*

Fortunately, by this time the lift had disgorged them into a quiet carpeted corridor, lined with scenes from the glory days of the Raj. Sue stopped outside the third door in the corridor, knocked quietly, waited and then opened it, ushering Andrew through before her. *"Mr. Davies for you, Mr. Mortby."*

The Colonel (as he obviously wasn't known here) drew back his chair and leapt to his feet to shake Andrew warmly by the hand. *"It's been a shamefully long time"* he began. *"Can I start to make amends with a very good dry sherry of my own that I bring in? The new rules don't exactly encourage alcohol consumption on the taxpayer so it's that or their ghastly tea. Come and sit down."*

Andrew thought the chair was probably a good deal older than he was himself. But it looked comfortable and that, he thought, was what counted on a Thursday evening after a long day. *"Yes, it has indeed been a long time – maybe 18 months. Should I call you Colonel by the way?"* *"Of*

4

course" his host replied *"Everyone here calls me that – to my face and behind my back. Now, Sue"* he went on, for she was still standing silent and unmoving by the door, *"you get off home. Just leave my overnight papers in the usual briefcase on your desk; and I'll catch up with you around 10 tomorrow."* Sue bobbed her head in quiet agreement, almost curtseyed as she left, and was gone.

The Colonel sat himself down in a chair that matched Andrew's and sipped his sherry. He was one of those men whose age it was impossible to guess accurately – Andrew thought he must be about 55. He had probably looked much like that ten years earlier. He was a man that Andrew had warmed to as soon as they had met. *"No side"* as one of his public school friends would have said. The Colonel certainly looked very comfortable in his own skin, very much in control of his life and work. Andrew had found him calming when they had first met, which was when Andrew had left the Army about five years ago and was about to join the bank he now worked for. Just as well, Andrew thought. If the man who was your controller – and thus a key figure in your life – was **not** relaxed and visibly in control, it would be pretty worrying.

The Colonel looked steadily at Andrew for some seconds. *"Andrew, you've probably and rightly guessed that we want something from you – to bring you out of retirement again. And, as this would only be the third time in five years, I hope that will be alright. This time, also, I think I can promise you some fun along the way."* Andrew muttered something conventional about always being available at need; after all, they did augment his salary by a modest but worthwhile amount each month. And, truth to tell, he had begun to find that his work at the bank was losing any intellectual or other attraction it might once have had for him.

The Colonel went on. *"What we're asking you to do this time is a bit vague – at least it is now. To cut straight to the chase, we want you to make yourself 'available' to a group that interests us. We want you to try and get into what passes for their management structure and tell us whether or not we should be worrying about what is going on. You won't know who; but we've already got a couple of people trying to do the same thing. But they're not making much progress – their backgrounds aren't attractive enough for the group. We think they will find you much more interesting. No danger for you, as far as we can see; and, as I say I think you'll have fun."*

"Sounds fine to me, as far as it goes." Andrew rolled what had turned out to be a very nice Amontillado appreciatively round his mouth. *"But who are we talking about? And why would I be of interest to them?"*

The Colonel paused so long that Andrew wondered if he should repeat his questions. Had the man heard? Just as Andrew was about to saying something, the Colonel did indeed respond. *"We're interested in the Angels. We think they are gearing up for a massive expansion in activity before the next Election. We know they are looking for able, well-educated and committed people with a business or at least project-management background. People like you. You are well-educated. You've held down a job that shows you can take responsibility and manage a project. Just as your Army background will appeal to them. They'll wet themselves when they find you can speak some Arabic; and wet themselves again when they find that* your dear old Catholic mother has produced a son who might understand half of the religious stuff they sometimes come out with among their own."

"Fine so far" replied Andrew. "But what are they doing that worries you? That in any way could carry the kind of threat to national security that I thought you guys are here to protect? From what I've read and heard, they are just a few hundred born-again Christians and left-wing drop-outs who offer love and consolation to anyone who will listen."

"That might have been true a year ago but things have moved on. A lot." The Colonel reached over and refilled Andrew's glass and then his own, without asking. As though no civilised person could possibly forgo a second glass at this time of evening. "They're opening new offices faster than Costa Coffee can open new outlets. And in the big Northern towns. They've probably upped their spending on their drug rehab programmes by 100% at the same time. We hear they have reached some deal with the Muslim Angels for the two groups to work together. And their income" the Colonel slapped the arm of his chair to emphasise the point "is now £100 million or more a year. You can keep quite a show on the road with that amount of money. If they ever were, they're no longer a bunch of religious do-gooders."

Andrew held up his hands, acknowledging the force of what the Colonel was saying. "OK. But what kind of cover story have you come up with for me? I don't want to screw up my position at the bank if I can help it. And presumably you need some kind of story for the Angels about why I might now be interested in them- and why I suddenly have time to help them?"

The Colonel smirked – it was the only way Andrew could describe it. "Yes, I think you'll find we have been rather clever for once. As soon as you agree to do this, one of the Gulf States is going to request your bank to second someone who has just your qualifications to them. That State is one your bank has been bending every sinew to get on the right side of, as they still have plenty of oil money. The secondment will be for six months initially but that can be extended if need be. The deal will be that you train a couple of their central bank people in the latest anti-money laundering rules the Financial Action Task Force has brought in. Most of that training can take place over here, at the State's London office; and I'm told you'd probably only need a day a week to supervise that. But the bank I'm sure will be happy to let you out full-time – so you'll have plenty of time for what we want."

Andrew admitted *"That is pretty clever. The bank will like it, providing the request comes from the Sheikh or one of his immediate coterie. I can do AML stuff in my sleep. Yes, I can get the Gulf secondees to work mostly by themselves. And everyone knows that the Gulf States all need to keep up with the latest international rules, especially now the Americans are so hot on catching international trading by Iranian companies. I shall need to spend a couple of weeks out in the Gulf at the start, to see how their current standards are applied. But then we should be away."*

The Colonel finished his glass, *"I hope you've got no emotional attachments you can't walk away from. From all I hear about the Angels their social life is pretty full-on and time-filling. And what I hear about some of the women, I rather wish I were 30 years younger and free to take this on myself!"*

Andrew finished his own glass and stood up. *"That all sounds like a good basis to start. I'm up for this. Life has been a little too predictable and dull for my taste, lately. There is no-*

one 'special'. And I'll go on trusting your calls – they've worked out fine for me so far. I'll wait to hear from the bank. Tell your Gulf Prince to emphasise the urgency of the work, so the bank will be a bit quicker to react than they would normally."

"As always, a pleasure to see you" said the Colonel. "Sue will still be here I expect. She doesn't trust me to lock up properly. I'll get her to escort you out."

2

It was actually three weeks before the secondment came through; and then two weeks while Andrew paid a visit to the Gulf to see for himself where they were already on Anti-Money Laundering. He used the time sensibly – clearing his diary and preparing training materials for his new charges. The latter was aided by the fact that the Financial Action Task Force had just produced two new volumes of rules and recommendations. While in the UK he also read all he could find on the Angels; and, as he thought about it, he could see that his proposed cover story would probably stand up very well.

The more he read about the Angels the less clear was the organisation. Its public face was that of an active and wide-ranging charity, an example of the 'Big Society' that David Cameron had talked about some years earlier.

It seemed to be split along three semi-autonomous lines. One was clearly aimed at single men and women under 25, with emphasis on social events and 'life-style' advice. A second was aimed primarily at mothers with young children, the emphasis here being on advice and support. A third was clearly aimed at the Saga generation, with lots of practical support on finance, ageing and health. Frequently, the offices of the three units– the Angels called them stores- were collocated in a town. After what had obviously been a rapid expansion in the last year, there now seemed to be a store in every major city in England, plus Edinburgh, Glasgow and Cardiff. There were few in rural areas.

Very little was said on the Angels' website about how the organisation was financed or administered, though it was apparent that much of the money came indirectly from two elderly brothers who, over the previous 20 years, had built up a major supermarket chain. Not only were they the source of the money but the chain, itself, which was nationwide, was also obviously used as a base for some of the Angels' charity work. Andrew himself had never shopped there; but he knew that –insofar as supermarkets can get good press – they were thought of in the same bracket as say the Co-Op had once been.

Andrew could also find relatively little on exactly what assistance individuals could expect if they made contact. Instead, there were numerous stories on social media from people claiming their lives had been transformed by their contact with the Angels. These came from drug addicts who described lengthy but successful cures; and mothers with young children who had found community, childcare and advice. Older people tended to focus on the health and finance aspects. There seemed to be a small network of medical experts with the organisation who came in for frequent electronic praise.

Andrew had to agree with the Colonel that here was an organisation which had access to considerable resources. Even allowing for the fact that many of the stores were probably transient rents of empty properties on High Streets, spending on property alone was clearly considerable. Most, if not all, the store helpers were probably volunteers, which again would cut the costs. But there must also somewhere be a significant back management layer who, if nothing else, would incur considerable running costs of their own. On the back of an envelope, Andrew reckoned that what he could see on the website alone might cost £5 million a month to run. The Colonel was right that there must be substantial funds somewhere.

The Angels' own PR was remarkably vague about the structure of the organisation, or its aims and how it was run. It referred to the 'fact' that much of the work was done by 'members' who subscribed to the principles that underlay the group. Andrew could find only three such principles:

- No discrimination of any kind;
- Do good and certainly do no harm;
- Belief, however vague, in any form of higher deity or God.

Andrew could see how the first two of these would play well with many groups in society. He was less sure about the third; but it turned out, on further digging, that the principle was set in very vague terms. He also found that, according to many surveys, up to 80% of the population as a whole believed in some form of Deity; and even among the young, if the question were asked the 'right way', that proportion was well over 50%. A staggering number also said they believed in angels, traditionally defined.

Beyond that, everything in the public domain put out by the Angels looked like the product of a confused 15 year-old. But Andrew realised that this might be deliberate and actually rather clever. The implication seemed to be that everyone was welcome to contact and use the Angels; but membership, or being on the 'inside', was by invitation. Andrew saw that he would need to obtain such an invitation, as soon as possible,

Andrew also looked, largely in vain, for critical pieces on the Angels by journalists or other investigators. Either they were squeaky clean or they had an extraordinarily good PR department who had kept negative comment to an absolute minimum. Several journalists had clearly done what Andrew intended to do – and presented themselves at an Angel store as individuals needing help. But most of these people said that they had then found themselves smothered in good intentions and caring people, a lot of talk and limited, though sensible, advice. No-one described 'brainwashing' or any form of political agenda or, indeed, anything that could be classified as abuse of the individual concerned. The nearest analogy he could come up with was of an organisation like the Salvation Army, but with money and without any seriously religious content. No wonder they had managed to get a decent press.

He did find some oblique references to the sexual proclivities of some Angels. It seemed they were split into two groups. For one of these, either sex was not for discussion or not relevant; and the other – gay and straight – were openly aggressive supporters of the lifestyle they claimed to follow. Any commentator who picked up on this then went on to say that the Angels had evolved signals by which people could recognise like-minded individuals and so avoid any awkwardness. Andrew decided without much thought that his physique and his Army and City backgrounds fitted only with the image of a testosterone-driven straight male. Nothing else would be plausible or, for him, enjoyable. Perhaps, Andrew thought, this was what the Colonel had been alluding to, when he had wished himself young enough to have taken on the job himself.

The Colonel's own organisation provided remarkably little of substance on the Angels. They explained this by saying they didn't want to prejudice Andrew's own views. But Andrew suspected that it was, in fact, the result of their having little to pass on.

3

Andrew realised that he had better get on and make the first move. That, he decided, should be a visit to one of the main High Street outlets, in Oxford Street. There, he would pose as a man with time on his hands, and a potential commitment to what the Angels said they were about. And he would see where that took him.

That decision was made on a Saturday. The following Monday found him standing outside the 'store' concerned, around 11 a.m. He had thought that Monday should be a fairly quiet day for the Angels and that anything earlier than mid-morning might seem strange. The store looked like it had been an HMV outlet, or something similar, in a previous life. The front to the street was wide and it had been contoured so that, in the windows, there was room for a large entrance to the left which merely said ' ANGEL SOCIAL' over it. To the right was another which just said 'ANGEL FAMILY'; and in the middle, inset, was a slowly moving escalator with signs indicating 'ANGEL HEALTH & FINANCE' up on the first floor. These were obviously the manifestations of the three branches of the Angels he had read about on the web.

Well, he had no doubt which he wanted so he pushed through the 'SOCIAL' entrance. He could see quickly that the store went in from the street quite some way. The front section seemed given over to garish boards identifying upcoming gigs, classical concerts, open parties, talks – the range seemed extensive. At the side were a series of booths, each with a small table and a tablet hooked in. The back of the store seemed to contain a number of enclosed areas – perhaps rooms where private stuff was discussed. Overall, it made for an informal, colourful, set-up. Space was largely taken up; but Andrew could see only a handful of people browsing the material so the effect was not stuffy or threatening. Andrew's eye then fell on a couple of spaces where a sign hung above them said 'ANGEL POINT'. It didn't take a genius to work out that this was where you probably went if you wanted to talk to one of the locals; and indeed at one of them a girl stood looking idly around. She was dressed quite smartly in a light green and informal jump suit; for some reason, Andrew had expected Angels to be in white but there was nothing wrong with green. He walked up to the girl, introduced himself and began to explain what he wanted. Her name tag indicated she was called Carol and she looked (and sounded) quite young, probably not long out of school.

"Carol" Andrew began. *"I hope I'm at the right place. I've heard a lot about the Angels. For reasons I won't go into now, I find myself with a few weeks' free time and thought it would be an ideal opportunity to find out more. To make myself known and see if I could make myself useful."* Carol smiled back at him, in the way one does, even if a volunteer, if your job involves talking to 50 people a day, 49 of whom you will never see again. *"Great"* she replied. *"We always need active doers. We have a simple routine that should help us tell you quickly what we can do for you and find out what we need to know about you."* She gestured at the side-wall. *"We've got a set of booths there. Take an empty one. Type 02 into the Tablet and it will come up with a short questionnaire about you, your interests, what we can do for you. You answer only what suits you in the Questionnaire. You can type your answers in or speak to the console on the wall, which is a speak-write. And that will then show your answers up on the form itself, on the screen for you to check the speak-write has got it right. Just type in or say 'END' when you've had enough; and we'll take it from there. Oh, and by the way, help yourself to coffee and muffin or cake on the way. We really have good coffee and of course it's free."* *"Sounds good"* said Andrew *"I'll give it a try."*

The system proved as easy as she had said it would be; and the coffee was better. Andrew still remembered with some nostalgic fondness the sign that had stood on the coffee table in the Catholic Church hall where he had spent many Sunday mornings in his youth. The sign had said simply *"Don't complain about the coffee – you'll be old and weak yourself one day."* And that was how Andrew typically felt about coffee in public places. The Angel coffee in contrast was in a totally different league and the small muffin he had grabbed almost as good.

The form had all the obvious – age, address, work history – and a few other less obvious things as well. But the system made clear you only had to answer what you wanted. And so rapid was the process that Andrew had reached the end of the form before reaching anywhere near the end of his patience. He thought briefly before signing off. He had managed to drag in the points that the Colonel had stressed would appeal to the Angels, such as his Catholic childhood, his Army experience and his knowledge of Arabic. Satisfied, he said *"END"* to the Tablet and returned to Carol.

She smiled at him. *"I've asked one of my senior colleagues, Chloe, to look at your input. If you could just hang on for 5 minutes, she'll be with you. Do look around while you're waiting. Whatever your tastes in music and in entertainment, I'm sure you'll find something of interest. Quite a few of the events shown here are not open to the public, so we can tell you immediately if something you're interested in is available. And coming to gigs is the way many people start to experience what we can offer."* With that, she moved off.

A new figure in green appeared by his side in less than 5 minutes and Andrew could see from her name tag that this was Chloe. She was older than Carol, maybe late 20s; and, while dressed in similar fashion to Carol, she somehow managed to make the ensemble come to life in a way that the other girl hadn't. Blonde hair and lots of it helped, as did her green-blue eyes which smiled – seemingly genuinely – at Andrew. She wasn't tall and she was slight in build – willowy with not an ounce of fat in sight. In fact, for Andrew, she quickly ticked most of his physical boxes for deciding whether a girl he had met was worth pursuing.

"What an interesting personal history, Andrew – may I call you Andrew?" she said. Without waiting for a reply, she went on. *"I'd love to find out more about why you're here and what we might be able to do for you but now isn't an ideal time. I'm having a get-together of relatively new people at a bar pretty near where I see you work – tomorrow night starting at 7. Do you think you could make that? I'd have plenty of time then and you get the chance to meet a few old and potential new Angels over a drink. Do say you'll come."* She smiled directly at him. Andrew felt that, even had it not been convenient, he could hardly turn down such a chance; and, of course, it was actually just the start he wanted. *"I'll be there."* he promised.

"Great" she replied. *"What I can do for you straightaway is to introduce you to Freddy. He knows far more about the Angels than most potential new recruits ever want to know. And I'm sure he can fill you in enough for you to get something worthwhile out of the drinks. I see you put your mobile number into your form. I'll send you the details for tomorrow. And see you then. Carol will find Freddy (really Frederick) and get the 2 of you together."*

4

Frederick turned out to be happy to answer to 'Freddy'. He was a lean, sparse man who might have been in his late 30s. From his style of dress, slightly long hair and a neatly trimmed, short beard, he gave the impression that he had started life as a hipster and got stuck somewhere early along the way. Andrew introduced himself but Freddy had obviously already been briefed and, within 2 minutes, they had moved to the back of the store. Andrew was seated and ready to start, fortified by his coffee and muffin.

"I understand from Clo that you may be better informed than some I talk to. So what exactly is it you want to know about the Angels?" Freddy began. Andrew had had no real chance to sum his new companion up and he realised now that Chloe had failed to brief him about Freddy. "I *suppose what I am really asking is are you people for real? And what is real in your world?"*

Freddy smiled to himself. *"Let's just go back a bit. And let me ask what does the word 'angel' conjure up for you?"* Andrew recalled his Catholic upbringing. *"Well, the word angel means messenger doesn't it? If I remember correctly, most of the Old Testament's relevant references are to messengers, which then got taken later to mean what we now think of as angels. Then, by the time you are in the New Testament you have angels proclaiming Jesus' birth, appearing after his death and so on. Finally, by the time you get to the Book of Revelations at the end of the New Testament you've got Archangels, angels, cherubim, heaven knows what else."*

"Pretty accurate, as far as it goes" Freddy replied. *"The Greek word giving rise to the word angel actually means messenger. But I'm not sure it's right to start with the Old Testament. Many of us think the Zoroastrians were the first to come up with the concept, in Ancient Persia; and it was taken on by the Jews in captivity there and turned into what you remember. But, yes, however it started, it's true that many of the references in the Old Testament were to messengers that could have been human or divine.*

What you perhaps don't know is that many other religions also have angels, or something very similar. This is a concept that clearly has resonance with humanity and is therefore a particularly helpful one for us. That's whether you're talking about Biblical Angels or things like individual Guardian Angels that popped up somewhere along the way. Many of us think we have come to give a big message to humanity, though we don't claim there is anything 'divine' about us. So the term Angels suits from several points of view."

Andrew felt he had to get back into this conversation. *"Well, I certainly remember that the Muslims have the same concept – didn't the Archangel Gabriel dictate the Qur'an to the Prophet? In a cave, wasn't it?"*

"You're right" said Freddy *"which, of course, is one reason why we've just managed to tie up a formal understanding with what are now known as the Muslim Angels. But there are other religions and cultures involved too. Japanese mythology has angel-like beings called Tennin and Tenshi. Baha'i literature has an angel-like creature usually called the 'Maiden of Heaven'; and so it goes on. All the way through to the Mormons – they too regard angels as messengers of God.*

In nearly all these cases, an angel is seen as something good, attractive and usually – though not always – androgynous, i.e. not obviously either male or female. Again, that all helps us with our public image. I say the word 'angel' and you immediately think of something pleasing to see, something 'special' and friendly."

Andrew interrupted again. *"What about the devil and 'fallen angels'? And what do you do about wings – which are something I suspect most people also factor into their image of an angel?"* Freddy smiled again. *"We're certainly not into adverts for Red Bull though, when someone becomes an angel, they do sometimes get given a set of wings as part of the ceremony. So, let's go easy on the wings, though we're kind of stuck with them, as are the Muslims – the Qur'an talks about angels with several sets of wings. But the image of Fallen Angels you mention is actually something we can and do make use of too. Everyone knows they fail to live up to expectations most of the time. In that way, they can think of themselves – with our help – as minor versions of 'fallen angels'. And most people seem to find it easier to think about evil if it's personified. So Satan really does have his uses. And we can use him too. If we ever get a serious problem with one of our own Angels – say for example they've had their hands in the till at work. Thankfully I can't think of anything like that; but there is then immediately a class, a type – the Fallen Angel, the instigator Satan – we could slot them into."*

Andrew decided that was more than enough theology for now. *"OK. Let's get onto the 'here and now'. What is this 'big message'? Where are you trying to take it?"* Freddy didn't seem put out by the directness of the question. *"Chloe's twittering won't have given you much idea – quite a lot of the Angels can't actually explain coherently what they're about. So let me do the intelligent tourist guide, which incidentally will help show why we think people like you need to be in our tent, not outside it. Indeed, that's why I'm spending this time with you now. I understand that one of the reasons why you're here is to help you decide whether you want to be 'in' or not. It's my job to help you get interested.*

First, and I'll be very frank, we intend to be a political party, albeit of a rather unusual kind. We're not a cult. Apart from belief in God (and, as you've probably worked out already, we're pretty relaxed about what constitutes 'God') we ask our members to agree only on two things. That the world needs improving; and that we each can help to make things better. There is an unspoken fourth element and that is that, whenever you are in doubt about the right course, you listen to Michael. I'll come back to him in a minute."

Andrew stayed silent and Freddy continued, this time talking so it seemed almost to himself. *"80% of the British say they believe in God, although only a couple of million actually ever go to a Christian church except for a wedding or a funeral; and maybe another couple of million plus are active*

Muslims or Jews. Most of the rest of this 80% are not religious in any active sense. But they do know that the world is a cruel and harsh place, one that they'd like to see changed. And, provided you don't push them too hard or too often; and provided you make it 'fun' to belong, there's a whole lot of people who will keep you company down what could for us be a long and winding road. What we have to do, over time, is convert that into votes at the ballot box.

We are immensely lucky to have someone, in Michael, who seems able always to articulate what that mass of people are likely to feel and who can lead them so that they think they're leading him. We're incredibly lucky to have the resources of the Foundation behind us; that gives us the money to make it 'fun' for so many people. For most of the people who do things with us, we're like a great club with no membership fee. One that you can join and leave pretty well at will. One that lets you find people you are likely to have something in common with – and have that fun, while at the same time often doing something that makes you feel proud to be part of the club."

Andrew shifted his weight to get more comfortable – the chair was at best utilitarian and with little padding. *"But that can't be all, can it? Who really calls the shots? Where is your 'long and winding road' supposed to go?"*

Freddy did bridle a little at this last remark and it was a few seconds before he turned to look Andrew in the eye and respond. *"There are perhaps 4,000 people who are 'angels' and who determine what the Angels do and where they should go. They are, if you like, the Founder Members chosen initially by Michael himself, though we've now got so big he has to delegate increasingly. Those 4,000 are the ones who roll up their sleeves and get their hands dirty if need be. They are the ones who organise and facilitate the cosy cuddly bits – all the counselling and support – but who also make and implement the hard decisions. Chloe isn't a typical Angel. She has just been around for years and she has put herself on the line for the Angels a number of times, so no-one here could doubt her commitment. She's one of the Inner Circle. Above them is a Council of Seven. You won't be surprised to know we call them Archangels; of whom one, Michael, is the centre, the key to everything. And 'no' his name isn't Michael. But with St Michael being just about the only Archangel any normal person could name, it was kind of obvious.*

Anyway" Freddy glanced at his watch *"you've probably had enough for one go. Come back sometime later in the week if you want. Now, I need to get your bands, so you won't be completely out of it if Chloe takes you out with her usual gang."*

Freddy rose, disappeared for around a minute and came back clasping a thin box about 20 cms in length. Freddy resumed his rather one-sided conversation. *"I've brought the bands I assume you'll want – you don't look either gay or a monk!"* Freddy opened the box. *"If you stay around, you'll find the Angels have a variety of bands of different types. But they all have just one purpose, to avoid any misunderstandings about sexual preferences. Clo goes with a pretty lively crowd so these are what you need. Wearing these, even though you're not an Angel, will help you get accepted by those who are."* Freddy produced three seemingly elasticated arm-bands about 2cm wide, discarding several others. *"These go below the elbow on your left arm. The top band you wear shows your sexual preference; white for straight, pink for gay, the two alternating if you swing both ways. I assume you will want white. The second band shows your sexual appetite. Light blue for 'willing and ready', dark blue for 'not interested' or 'not now'. I'll give you both of those. The third is designed to show your current involvement with anyone else. If you're going with another Angel or an ordinary partner, and not interested in anything else then it's black. If you're open to offers then it's green. Again I'll give you both but I would point out that Angels who are out on the razzle take it pretty badly if they proposition someone with a green band and that person then turns them down. That'll get you through one night with Clo's friends. Just think what bands you want before you go out, not during! And remember to get the order of the three right if you don't want to look stupid."*

5

Andrew got a text from Chloe about 10 a.m. the next morning. The suggested venue was only about 10 minutes' walk from Andrew's apartment – a pub where Chloe's message said that the Angels often met with newish members. Andrew had a relaxed, free, day. He took considerable care over his wardrobe for the evening. The weather was fine and warm enough for him not to need to wear a jacket. The main problem was finding a shirt the colour of which would fit aesthetically with the three bands Andrew intended to display – white, light blue and green. He was, at least grateful that the persona he needed to adopt and his preferences coincided. But he realised that, if he got accepted within the Angels, he might have to splash out on some new shirts of suitable background colour. In the end, his choice for the evening settled on a light yellow which did not show the white off to advantage but did blend into the background for all three bands.

The text had said 7 p.m., presumably designed for people working locally but who worked for banks which typically expected the middle and back office staff at least to stay well after 6. The bar chosen was unremarkable but not hard to find. And at around 7.10 Andrew walked into the main bar area. There were enough people there to make it seem active but not overcrowded. No doubt the set that typically dived into a bar for a 'quick one' on the way home had already left for their suburban commute. At one end of the bar, Andrew quickly located Chloe in a small group of ten or so. Now he knew what to look for, he could see that only three including Chloe were displaying bands. The others looked rather like him in age and dress. Presumably possible new recruits who were being introduced to their first taste of Angel life.

He caught Chloe's eye and she made room for him, asking at the same time *"what would you like to drink? Most of us are trying the excellent range of gins they have on offer here."* Andrew said that would suit him very well and Chloe organised a glass for him.

Andrew had already decided to stay as schtum as possible, to see how things were handled. He quickly established that there were two conversations in train, one a typical review of the life of over-worked young people having to commute long distances. The second – led by Chloe – was on something Michael had apparently recently been talking about, the need to clean up modern politics. Safe ground with people like this thought Andrew and he was right; Chloe had little difficulty leading her 'group' into a denunciation of all things associated with modern Government; and she did seem genuinely interested in the range and weight of points made to her by the sub-group she had. Every 15 minutes or so, another round of drinks appeared on the bar but no money seemed to change hands.

Over time, Andrew was able to chat briefly to the other two Angels, both girls. One worked in the Oxford Street store and was clearly new to the scene. The other introduced herself as Vivienne *("call me Vy")*. And she was much more interesting – dark haired, athletic and striking if not classically pretty. Andrew was quickly able to establish that she was a single mother who lived in an Angel commune.

Vy explained it this way. *"There I was with a 3 year old, no man. I needed somewhere where I could get good childcare and still be able to earn a living. There was this Angel group, about 30 women in the same boat, roughly two-thirds of who went out to work, the rest minded the children. I became one of the two-thirds. You pay in about half your net earnings, to give the childminders some income and pay for food and the group's expenses. And my little daughter now has so many 'mothers' she knows and trusts that I often feel she doesn't need me at all!"* After a little prodding by Andrew, it became apparent that this was just one of many such communes – each almost self-sufficient after the Angels had bought the initial property – and clearly, he thought a potential hotbed of pro-Angel sentiment and recruitment.

An hour – four drinks – later Andrew was starting to

feel light-headed and in need of food, when Chloe spoke up over both groups *"Right, time I let you all get home. It'll be £20 a head"* which to Andrew, who knew his way round City bars, was at least 50% under the normal going rate for what they had had.

As they spilled out onto the street, Chloe took the lead. *"Same time next week, if you want. I'll arrange somewhere to eat next time and I'll bring a couple of our gig organisers along so you can find out what's coming up that you might enjoy."* People started to head off, mostly alone though one couple left arm-in-arm. Andrew, of course, didn't know if they had arrived that way too. When it was just Andrew and the three Angels, Chloe smiled at him and said *"we often eat at the Thai round the corner. Do join us and you can ask a few of the questions I suspect are buzzing round your brain."*

Andrew said that would suit him well and they were soon seated in a pleasant small local restaurant, being fussed over by a small Thai national who clearly knew Chloe well. A short but lively discussion followed on the respective merits of green and yellow curry. When they had ordered food and Singhas each, Andrew thought he had better take his chance.

"Well now, first question – what was with the charging back there? Four generous gins each don't cost £20. Is that one way you guys start to introduce people to the joys of associating with angels – by giving them discounted drinks?" *"Well yes and no"* replied Chloe. *"You're right that the cost to the public would have been higher. But this is one of the ways in which we offer a good time for people who come into our orbit. We have a small book of pubs, restaurants and the like*

where anyone with Angel connections can get discounts; and nearly always this is because the owner has sympathies with us or knowledge of us and anyway offers discounts to get more business. So we don't need to end up subsidising the drinks. If we did, I guess even the Foundation would run out of money pretty quickly. In a restaurant like this, where the owner is himself an Angel, we shall be hard put to get him to accept any money at all but Vy can be quite hard-nosed when she wants. So you are about to enjoy a really good meal and it will cost you roughly half what a member of the public would pay. Think of it as another Angel benefit."

"Where did the kids at the drink come from? asked Andrew. This time it was the younger girl who chipped in. *"I've met all of them over the last 10 days just going round, being in places and making it clear I was an Angel. These are all people who have heard something about us and like at least some of what they hear; but who want to understand a bit more about us before any commitment. A bit like you, perhaps, according to Chloe."*

"OK, fine" replied Andrew. *"So, people like you gather up potential recruits in various ways, and then start off selling them some of the benefits of being with Angels, like cheap alcohol and cut-price gigs. Then what happens?"* *"There's no set pattern"* replied Vy. *"Some of them will stick around, come to a few gigs or a rave, maybe bring a few friends. And that's how they will get to know us. One in 10 of them perhaps will get much more involved – maybe like me because the Angels offer something (like a decent home environment) they need. The Angels anyway are a great dating agency. And, for this group of people, the emphasis is on being 'fun'. That's what most of these people lack, in their work-ridden commuter existence. Go North*

and you'd find the same kind of programme but with important local tweaks in Manchester, Birmingham, wherever."

Andrew felt he'd better not show too much interest beyond what he had already done, so the evening then moved into a relaxed, jokey phase. Chloe had been right. At the end, she had managed to press £25 a head on the very reluctant owner but only that after a heated debate and Chloe promising to bring another, larger, group very soon.

They spilled out into the street. It was now about 10.30 – the evening had gone very pleasantly thought Andrew. *"Hope you've enjoyed your first outing with us"* said Chloe to Andrew. *"Look out for a text from me very soon about what next – if we still interest you"* she added with what Andrew thought a very obvious smile round her lips. *"Yes, thanks"* said Andrew *"it's been fun."* And with that he turned away to walk back to his flat which was at most 15 minutes leisurely walk – enjoyable in this weather.

He had got only about 10 yards down the road when a female arm looped through his left arm and Vy appeared by his side. *"It's a bit late for me to get back to the Commune – we have a kind of deal where we try to avoid waking the smaller children by coming back when they're sound asleep. Chloe says your flat is near. Would you like some company tonight? I can see the colour bands on your arm match mine; and I can only assume someone explained to you what they mean."* *"Yes"* said Andrew *"Freddy back at the Oxford Street store, though I didn't expect them to get called into use quite this quickly."* Vy squeezed his arm. *"You were probably hoping it would be Chloe not me – I've seen you watching her when you thought no-one was looking. But I'm afraid I've never known her go*

32

with a man who wasn't an Angel. I'm not so fussy; my tastes are broad and my reviews are very good."

Andrew thought that, even if he had not actually felt the urge to accept her offer, which he did, he should probably go with it. He was trying to get accepted by the Angels, here was one throwing herself at him. *"I'll just send a text to the house mother who's on duty for my kid tonight to let her know I won't be back. And then let's go and have some fun."* Which Andrew had to admit the next morning was exactly what then happened.

6

Vy didn't hang around in the morning. She was up by 7 and, having made coffee for them both, she was very business-like, kissed him and left by 7.45. *"My office like me to be in by 8.30"* she said *"And I always keep a change of clothes there, so that's alright. I like your flat and I enjoyed you. Let's get together again some time if you like – but leave it a few weeks; I don't do regular dates."*

Andrew lay in bed for a bit relaxing. He probably shouldn't have had her back last night. But what else could he have done? And surely it would help him get to be accepted within the Angels? Anyway, he'd enjoyed it. Eventually, he got up, had a long relaxing shower and took himself off to a local coffee bar. Despite the ads on its windows, he couldn't help but compare the coffee and muffin he bought there unfavourably with what he had enjoyed at the Angel store two days earlier. And the latter hadn't cost him £6.50.

While he was finishing up, he checked his mobile, to find a message from Chloe. *"Vy says she had a good night and she thinks u're OK. I've been on to Michael and he says u sound interesting, he'd like to meet u soon. I'm attending a weekend away with him this Saturday and Sunday. If u're free, I'll pick u up from your flat, say 2pm Friday. Go and see Freddy, to get briefed"*

Andrew didn't have to think long about his answer. This was just what he wanted and it was unbelievably lucky that it had happened so quickly; no point in playing hard to get. So he texted back that he would see her on Friday around 2. The only bit he wasn't quite so happy over was the news that Vy had obviously been talking. Did Angels not understand some things were private?

The invitation certainly gave shape and purpose to Andrew's day. He needed to get back, contact Freddy and find out whatever he could about what he might expect at the weekend. About 3 p.m. therefore – he had decided there was little point trying to track Freddy down in advance, as he didn't have contact details – Andrew was back at the Oxford Store. He quickly established that yes Freddy was around; and, after what already seemed like the inevitable offer of free coffee, it was only about 20 minutes before Andrew found himself again on the uncomfortable chair near the back of the shop, with Freddy.

Freddy sat down and his opening remark made Andrew even crosser with Vy. *"I see your first evening with Chloe's lot went well. Vy's written up a very positive account of you. You'll find quite a few of the girls who go for new men like you will be in touch. Just choose wisely and sparingly would be my advice; but then you'd probably say I'm jealous."*

Andrew was cross. *"I thought Vy had a job. Obviously it doesn't stop her ringing all and sundry to gossip about me the morning after."* Freddy laughed. *"That isn't how it works – obviously no-one told you. What all the Angels do is keep an open diary online– what they've been doing, who they've been seeing, what they're thinking. And someone like me, who knows a lot of them, can just read through their daily thoughts. Anyway, Vy did more than just write briefly about you. One of the great innovations here is that Angels now always write up any shared experiences in full, scoring their partners – if they have one – out of 10. One of the great benefits is that any sign of 'undesirable' habits, liking non-normal sex for example, gets written up. Every future prospective partner from then on afterwards will know what to expect – indeed, whether to go out with them at all."*

Andrew felt angrier still. *"What happens if someone lies or misrepresents what happens? Doesn't the partner – me in this case – get to put the record straight if it's wrong?"* *"Well that's why every encounter gets written up. First, most Angels lean over backwards to be nice and fair-minded. If not, that's the kind of word that gets round the circuit and will damage the Angel's reputation with exactly those people the Angel wants to be liked by. Second, you ignore the odd critical remark. But if say three partners in a row record similar things, it's pretty obvious there's a potential issue. And, believe me, it's a great way for an individual – boy or girl – to check out partners in advance. Especially valuable I'm told in some of the more esoteric areas of sex. And, if you do have any 'quirks' in your sexual preferences,* it also means that anyone who still fancies you can focus right in."

Andrew thought he had heard enough for now. "Listen, Freddy, I haven't come to discuss my recent sex life. Chloe says Michael wants to meet me and she's taking me away to some week-end retreat, to do just that. What do I need to know?"

"You're very honoured" replied Freddy. "Chloe must really have laid it on with Michael about you. Well, I'm not privy to what the great people get up to. What I can tell you is that we have a number of out of town places –usually where something else goes on regularly, drug or alcohol rehab for example. And Michael uses some of these to hold policy-fests – where he discusses what the next stage of the overall plan needs to be. I suppose he's decided to let you sit in on the edge of one of these fests, so he can get a sight of you; and hopes you will come away fired up with the latest Angel thinking and having met an amazing man.

As to what you need to know, I guess my main advice would be to stick with Chloe and, if in doubt, ask her help. The only other thing I can probably usefully do is sketch who might also be there, that is if it is really a senior meeting.

If it is, what you are likely to find are several of the High Council of Seven, the people – six plus Michael – who really determine what's happening. The Angels may look all cosy and nice. But believe me, there is a huge amount of 'paddling under the water' to keep things moving. And fortunately the High Council is stuffed with people well able to pick up and see through the most complicated of plans. All the High Council are known within our group as Archangels and I'd better run through them for you. But don't take the names too seriously; most of them have nicknames even to their faces."

Freddy went on *"The basic problem is that all the Biblical references and bits from other religions don't give us many names of the supposed Archangels. And most of the ones there are grate terribly on modern ears. Apart from Michael, the only one who is widely known to any ordinary person is Gabriel; and even that is tricky because we have 2. One is Jibril – the Muslim name for Gabriel. He is a Muslim man and responsible for our links with the Muslim Angels. The other, Gabriel, is actually a girl, Gabrielle –I should say woman, she's a real ball-breaker – who everyone calls Gabby to her face. That actually helps with the Muslims, who couldn't bring themselves to have a female Archangel representing them, any more than they would want a male, non-Muslim Gabriel. In reality, Gabby runs finances. I don't think Angels in the Bible ever had to worry about things like money, so there's no Biblical source for that. And she acts as Michael's Number 2.*

That leaves 4 and that's where it gets messy, I should say 'debateable'. If you're that way inclined and don't have much of a life, you can actually go away for a weekend with like-minded Angels to debate subjects like 'John Milton and the naming of the Fallen Angels' or 'was Azrael an Archangel?' But I assume that's not to your taste. So, in short, let's just say the 4 names Michael settled on were:

- Raphael, which supposedly means 'God Heals' so he covers all aspects of health and personal wellbeing. You'll come across a lot of references to 'Rafa' (after the tennis player) if you ever get involved with any of the rehab centres we run;

- Uriel. Uri's associated with fire and justice, so think of him covering everything to do with law and order;

- Ariel, the name for the traditional patron saint of animals and the environment. So guess what, he covers all environmental

issues. And – despite how little you seem to know about the Angels – even you will probably have heard some of the Angel propaganda on global warming and the like.

- finally Sammy – actually Chamuel, the one who sees God. Ours is a woman who everyone calls Sammy, even to her face. Think of her as the Minister of Peace and a kind of glorified agony aunt rolled into one. Again, one tough lady but very good value."

"You talk about these people like they're a Cabinet in waiting, Ministers with different portfolios." said Andrew. *"Not far from the truth"* replied Freddy. *"Think of Michael as the CEO and Executive Chairman, the others are just like Ministers; and you won't be far wrong. Gabby is really Michael's Number 2 and, as I said, she runs the finances. And, although The Foundation has deep pockets, my guess is that money must be becoming a big issue, as our efforts expand across the country and into so many new areas. So, more power to her elbow. Last time I heard, for example, we had opened 60 rehab centres across the big cities in the last 18 months, mostly providing detox environments for alcohol or drug abuse. Very good they are – I'm told – not an area I hope ever to have to worry about personally. But that sort of thing comes expensive when nearly everyone who ends up there is just an ordinary person – usually an under 30 whose cure is being paid for 100% by us.*

Anyway, if you're being honoured by a weekend with some of these people, you'll probably know more than I do by Monday. What I can tell you from personal experience, Michael loves to sit around and talk about future policy. He likes to drag people out of whatever day-dream they're in and come up with viable policies in the areas that concern us and which are going to be critical as we go nation-wide. But my advice is to take it as it comes and trust Chloe – she's pretty straight and artless in her way of handling people. She won't deliberately land you in anything you can't handle.

Certainly, make sure you enjoy your weekend. The highlight will be the first time you sit and talk with Michael. Almost everyone who does so comes away believing that the difficult is possible and the impossible will get tackled just around the corner. It took me about two years to make the trip you're going on now, so forgive me if I sound a little jealous, because I am. Time with Michael must be the best thing on this grotty planet. It's over a year since I saw him and, on my good days, I can still face anything thrown at me, just by thinking of him."

7

By Thursday evening, Chloe had texted to say that she would pick Andrew up from his flat about 2 p.m. on Friday. He was to wait outside the apartment. Andrew decided to chill Thursday night. A couple of hours of not too strenuous gym work and swimming, plus a few beers and a take-away, did that for him very effectively. And he was asleep by 11.

On Friday morning, he gave some careful thought to what he should wear and take with him. He decided he had better trust Freddy's view that much of the time would be taken up with policy sessions round a table so 'dress down' seemed the order of the day. But he added one decent shirt and some chinos just in case. It was late August and the weather seemed set fair so Andrew didn't bother with any wet weather gear.

Time hung on his hands the next morning and Andrew was grateful when the clock crawled round to 2 p.m. and he could stand in the road and await Chloe. She was only about 10 minutes late, driving a non-descript Ford Escort of some years' vintage. She pulled up alongside him, indicated he should throw his case on the back seat and get into the front passenger seat. All of which he did without a word.

"Hello" she said as she pulled out. *"I'm so glad you could make this. The chance to spend time with Michael doesn't come very often, even for people like me. And it looks like a beautiful weekend."* *"Where are we going?"* asked Andrew. *"And what's actually going to happen?"*

"Well" she replied *"we're going to an Angel place in the country near Letchworth, so the journey shouldn't be too long. It's basically a drug rehab clinic but Michael has a kind of weekend retreat added on at the back. I think the Angels have perhaps a dozen such retreats around the country; and Michael travels round, encouraging the troops and planning the next stage in the campaign. He likes his whereabouts to be a bit of a mystery, so hardly anyone knows where he is at any point in time; and the logistics of keeping up with him must be a nightmare for the people responsible. Still, that's not my worry thank goodness. I'm just one of the old guard he likes to have around occasionally. He's sweet. He says people like me have a common touch and understand what ordinary people are thinking, which is what he needs to know. That could be pretty dismissive; but the way he puts it always makes me feel great, glad to be 'ordinary' and really wanted."*

She looked quickly across at Andrew. *"I see you've got your bands on. Those can go. It's not that kind of a weekend,* business not pleasure. And, whatever you do, never make a pass at any of the women around Michael. They regard looking after him as some kind of religious duty – we call them the Nuns (but not to their face, where they are Sisters). They travel with him and all the cooking and facilitation of the weekend will be thanks to them. So, be grateful, be nice but above all hands off!"

"Are they Michael's women?" Andrew asked. "Oh no" replied Chloe. "He gave that kind of thing up years ago. Which is a great shame. I managed a few nights with him about 5 years ago when he was still interested; and they were the best nights of my life. But, now, he's kind of risen above all that, though he absolutely doesn't want or expect others around him to do the same. The only thing he is adamant about is the use of contraceptives. I'm sure Vy had some with her the other night – that would be thanks to Michael always going on about it."

Andrew was not happy to hear that last remark. "You bloody women. Has every Angel read Vy's blog? First Freddy, now you. Makes me feel a fool." "You'll get used to it" commented Chloe. "And you'll find there are some really good aspects to it. If you ever became an Angel then the shared blogs are a way in which, within months, you can get to know and trust hundreds, if not thousands, of your colleagues. Tell me how you would do that – in the bank where you work for example. And trust among Angels is absolutely critical. There are so few of us for what needs to be done. How can anyone do their job properly if they can't trust and rely on the people around them? Of course, that doesn't mean everything always goes swimmingly. But you **do** know, if something goes wrong that might impact you, the Angel concerned will own up to the problem straightaway and ask for help. It's part of the culture – own up to problems as soon as you see them. That's what trust comes down to."

Chloe drove in a relaxed but not passive way. The miles got eaten up pretty quickly, especially once they escaped the M25. Andrew didn't initiate much conversation – he didn't feel in a position to do that. What he did establish was that they would arrive, Chloe would hand him over to the Sisters; and Michael would almost certainly talk to him privately before the first session, which would be over dinner and after. Chloe was bubbling at the prospect of spending time with people she obviously knew and liked. *"I can't tell you exactly who'll be there"* she said. *"But I expect at least 2 of the High Council will be with us, probably Gabby and one other. And the rest – maybe a dozen in all – will be from the Foundation, or a handful from the big Northern cities, a few of whom I'll know. Michael's always saying that one of the worst features of how things have been run in Britain for decades has been the over-reliance of policy on what London and the South-East want. As you'll no doubt hear, he doesn't think much at all of recent governments and politicians either!"*

Andrew knew they had arrived when Chloe slowed down and turned left up a narrow track. At the junction there had been a relatively small sign saying 'Start Over' Hotel, but otherwise nothing to indicate what was there. The narrow road broadened out after about half a mile and Andrew could see signs pointing to the car park. That had a couple of other cars and two minibuses parked. Chloe pulled up and they got out.

Andrew immediately felt drawn to the place. It was so peaceful. There were a surprising number of flowers around; and the sound of a few birds singing in the nearby trees. A typical country scene but one that straightaway conjured up the feeling that you were miles from the rat-race or any other part of the 'real world'.

Chloe took out her case, Andrew picked his up. Chloe obviously remembered the way because she headed for a fairly narrow gap in the nearby hedge and went through. *"The rehab building is the other way. You won't see it or its current inhabitants on this trip, though Michael will go and talk to them at some point I'm sure. The retreat is quite separate here at the back. I don't know what you're used to – I would call it comfortable without being flash."*

They walked down the path about 30 yards, which then turned sharply right. There, through a waist-high iron gate, Andrew could see a low two-storey brick building facing them. Before it was a small garden, where Andrew could see not much more than a patch of rough lawn with a handful of benches scattered over it. Also, a couple of rose beds, standards and mostly well past their prime for this year. Chloe cut across the small lawn, making for the clearly-defined entrance. *"All the action takes place on the Ground Floor"* she called over her shoulder to Andrew. *"It's just bedrooms and store rooms upstairs."*

As they reached the door, it swung open and a middle-aged woman stepped out to meet them. She wore a slightly severe dark blue long skirt and a light blue shirt that went well with it. No make-up or any other ornamentation save for a small simple silver cross on a chain around her neck. *"Hello, Sister"* said Chloe walking towards her, dropping her case and embracing her warmly. *"I might have guessed that you'd still be looking after Michael. It's wonderful to see you again."* Chloe turned to look back at Andrew who was standing perhaps two metres behind the pair of them. *"This is Sister Valerie who runs absolutely everything. She's the go-to person for anything you may want while you're here."* Andrew stepped forward and shook Valerie's proffered hand. *"I'm pleased to be here"* Andrew said *"though a bit bowled over by everything being so new to me." "Say no more"* Valerie's voice was deep and restful, in total agreement with the atmosphere that seemed to permeate the whole environment. *"I'm sure Chloe can remember where we serve tea for people as they arrive. She can also show you your room – you are in Number 3, she is in 4. They're all en-suite. And we don't bother with things like keys – you'll find out that's the Angel way. So, have some tea, and go and unpack."* She glanced at her watch. *"It's about 4 now. Michael has asked to see you around 6, Andrew. One of us will come and get you from your room when it's time. Prayers and food will be about 7."*

Chloe took them to get some tea. There was no-one else around. She then led him upstairs to Room 3 which held a bed, chair and table, chest of drawers and built-in wardrobe plus a small bookcase with perhaps 30 books in it. Andrew could immediately see a Bible on the shelf, together with what looked like devotional books of the kind he associated with his Catholic childhood. But he was relieved to see also at least a dozen books by authors like Michael Connolly and CJ Sansom. So, without checking further, Andrew thought he could probably find something to read if need be. Chloe smiled up at him. *"I'll leave you to it. Do walk if you feel like it, you can't get lost. And, if not before, Prayers around 7."*

8

It took Andrew just 10 minutes to unpack and explore his room and the rest of the top floor. He had been trained always to seek out the Fire Exit, which he did. Otherwise, there seemed nothing of interest. He decided to stay in his room and just enjoy the restful atmosphere. His eyes may have closed because, when Sister Valerie came for him just before 6, he definitely didn't register her presence in the room until she spoke. *"Michael's downstairs. I'll show you to the room."*

Andrew followed her down the stairs and into a large room opposite, on the Ground Floor. Andrew tried to take in where he was. The room was very large – it must have been several rooms at one time that had now been knocked together. There were various sizes and types of chair facing inwards, which together gave

Andrew the impression that he might have walked into the Senior Common Room at an Oxbridge College. A rather imposing fireplace stood at one end though, given the weather, this was empty. Andrew realised this room must be where the policy sessions would be held.

Michael was standing motionless in front of the empty fireplace. He had already half turned towards the door and, as Andrew entered, he moved forward a couple of paces towards Andrew and held out his hand. *"Welcome, I'm so glad you could come. I just hope we will have enough 'entertainment' for you to make your weekend enjoyable. Please sit down and let's talk."*

Andrew reached for one of the single chairs and sat. Michael found a chair almost opposite but not so close that Andrew felt in any way under pressure. Now that his brain was working properly, Andrew realised that Michael himself was not a particularly impressive figure. Roughly the same height and build as Andrew himself. Maybe late 30s or older, with a luxuriant head of black curly hair and sparkling eyes in a face that looked as though it regularly broke into smiles or laughter. In short, very unintimidating, not at all what Andrew had projected though, now he thought of it, he wasn't sure what he had really expected. Michael was also dressed very much as Andrew himself. No sign of a monk's cassock or anything to mark him out as someone special. But what he did have – and what Andrew felt the moment he had touched his offered hand – was a sense of calm, power and personal wellbeing, which seemed to flow from him and fill the space around him. Andrew could feel that well-being spread up his own arm and warm his whole body. Against his own better judgment, Andrew was impressed.

"I found the brief CV you gave when you visited the Oxford Street store last week very striking" Michael said. *"As you can probably imagine, we don't get that many obviously talented people turning up each week saying they might be interested in working with us. Though, Heaven knows, we need plenty, especially now. Certainly, we don't get many people like you who have held down tough Army and then private sector roles or who can speak a difficult language like Arabic with apparent ease. Tell me a bit more."*

Andrew had expected to be quizzed on his CV and had thought carefully through how best to present himself, to conform to the cover story he had. Fortunately, one of the Colonel's astute moves, the CV *was* genuine, so Andrew had no trouble talking briefly about his education, his Army career or his move into investment banking via a spell in the Middle East. What was more difficult, he thought, was how best to give Michael the impression that he, Andrew, was up for taking on something interesting for the Angels, without seeming to throw himself at them.

He found himself saying in conclusion *"So, I've got this few months – effectively a paid Sabbatical from the bank while I think about what I want to do with the rest of my life. I'm not short of money. The people I'm supervising should only need a day or so a week of my time. My parents both died when I was quite young, and I've still got the great bulk of what they've left me. So, I'm not short of cash. I'd heard a bit about what you Angels are up to and thought, well, perhaps you might have something worth my turning a hand to – preferably something very different from what I've done so far."*

"Understood" replied Michael. *"in the sense that, from this and your CV, I think I see the kind of things you could do for us, what you would be good at; and what also might broaden your horizons. But, before we go there; if you are to be of real use and to last the pace, you need to hear and believe in what we're up to. And you need to see just why I think you might bring something extra and different for us. Volunteers are great. Volunteers who start to understand their role in the wider picture and can internalise that have far more drive and value to us. I'm really only happy when I have people around me who can see that wider picture.*

First, where we are going. As you probably know we are within 14 months of an Election. You need to believe that, in that time, we can create a sufficiently wide national political movement that, at the Election, we can get a large number of MPs voted in. We firmly intend to capture the government of this country. We're not going to be like UKIP in 2015, nearly 4 million votes and just 1 MP. Think much more of examples like Emmanuel Macron in France who created a party out of almost nothing in under a year and won the Presidential Election there in 2017. Trump in the US at the end of 2016 was another example – at least evidence that someone 'new' can take on and defeat the power machines that run political parties everywhere – even someone like him. There have been plenty of other examples elsewhere in Europe too- the Five Star Movement in Italy for one.

How do we think we can do this? Well, I would say we have four great advantages – over say Macron in 2016. The first is money. You probably don't know much about the size and source of our finances. But I can promise you that they are substantial and that I have been laying the groundwork (and putting money by) now for 4 years. We will be by far the best financed party contesting this upcoming Election. And money can fill in many of the gaps that even good party machines tend to have.

Second, ideas. At present, most outsiders who know anything about us think of some kind of giant charity. And so, in a way, we are. But every home we create for single women with families, every rehab class we offer for people on drugs or alcohol, every counselling service we provide to the elderly and the financially insecure can be thought of as something quite different. They are, in fact, living examples of what we could and will do if we can get control of the vast amounts of public money that get spent now in these areas. In other words, we can already demonstrate that our policies are likely to work if they can be tried on a bigger stage. Most of the other political newcomers, elsewhere, have had only promises to offer.

Third, novelty together with a typically British style of nostalgia. We are 'new people'. No more tired established politicians with their endless expenses, sexual harassment and other comet trails of grief behind them. The ordinary voter is sick and tired of being lied to; so we will make it a priority to tell the truth and nothing else. As for nostalgia, how often do you hear people, especially older people, long for the days when the country was relatively at peace with itself? Life before BREXIT and before the Labour Party started tearing itself to shreds wasn't the joy-ride people remember. But we think we can remind people that we're all in this together; that there needs to be what some would call in 'old-speak' a new social contract.

And we think we can deliver that to an electorate that is suspicious, tired of experts. Voters' dissatisfaction with the old *way of doing things has been the key supporting factor behind the success of new parties in a large number of EU countries. We will have new faces, clean hands, policies and procedures that we are prepared to share in advance and live by in the event.*

Compare that with the other national parties. The Tories still at daggers drawn with each other over what happened up to BREXIT. Labour, with a Leader that half of them would turn their backs on given the chance. Even the death of the Queen has made change easier to contemplate; the periods after Elizabeth 1 and Victoria were both marked by significant and rapid political change. You can sense that people already half-expect that pattern again. After Victoria, we had most of the political growth of a new party, Labour. In a sense all we Angels will be trying to do, just over a century later, is replicate the emergence of a new party again. And, as almost everything can happen now much faster than it did a century ago, why not us in 14 months?

Finally, my fourth point, we have a potential army with numbers, energy and who are fed up – the younger voters. I've touched on how we might appeal to older voters – though we have to be realistic and recognise it's no easy thing to change the voting habits of a person's lifetime. Again, most of the upheavals – from France through the Middle East and into Asia – have been driven by young people who have two priceless commodities in abundance – energy and technical savvy. The Angels already have close connections with tens of thousands of young people who think positively of us and whose energies I am sure we can harness. The next Election will take the use of technology in politics to new levels. No party is as well placed as we are to find and use the technology that can be deployed. Anyway, enough from me before this becomes an Election speech. How am I doing so far?"

Andrew took a little time to order his thoughts and reply. His first, internal, thought had been how pleased the Colonel would be when he, Andrew, could report on all this – obtained straight from the horse's mouth. He finally said *"Well let's suppose that the finances are really there, that policies are set out and already partially in place; and that there is an embryonic network of people out there ready to 'go at your command'. I can see that you might then really have a lot to build on, quickly and in substance. Though I would still think your biggest hurdle is going to be binding together the disparate rowing factions across the country into accepting something more like give and take."*

"Very fair comment" Michael said. *"Now, I need to find a way to test out your abilities to help us – and, at the same time, let you see that you really would bring significant strengths to the party. We also need to give you the chance to see that the lynchpins for progress that I've been talking about really are there. Let me think. We'll come back to all that at the end of the weekend, if we may."*

Michael looked at his watch. *"About 20 minutes to Prayers – which means 22 minutes to food! I'm sure Chloe will be sitting somewhere in the front garden enjoying this lovely weather. I suggest you go and find her and I'll join you soon. After food, the policy session will start. You will be welcome to sit in and listen – but don't feel under any compulsion to stay. We don't do 'polite' here."*

9

Andrew found Chloe sitting in a patch of warm sunshine on one side of the garden. Eyes closed, face raised to the sun. Not for the first time, Andrew thought how beautiful she was, especially in repose like this. The combination of her good looks and the very obvious fact that she was at peace with herself was, he found, irresistible.

He stood quietly and watched her for a minute and then she gave a start and came to. *"You"* she said. *"Must mean you've talked to Michael. Is it time to eat? Have you heard a bell?"* She rose and put her arm in his, one of the first intimacies he could remember from her. *"Sit next to me when we go in."* She checked quickly with her watch. *"I'll make sure you don't foul up too much. When you meet people, just nod to show you've recognised they are there. There'll be introductions later. If you do have any food allergies, grab one of the Sisters and explain. It's amazing what they can conjure up, as there will be vegan dishes, gluten-free food and so on already mixed in with what you'll see. If you don't have any allergies, just follow your nose. Try a bit of everything you fancy and go back for more when you're ready. It's all self-service. And there will be wine and beer on the side for those who need it!"*

At that point, a gong – not a bell – could be heard, emanating from the room Andrew had recently left. Chloe led him back in. Even in the few minutes he'd been outside, the room had been transformed. Tables were now covered with large tablecloths and two had food warmers on them – very obviously, by their look and smell, with a range of interesting things to eat. Huge salad bowls, olives, cheese, great hunks of French bread completed the picture. Andrew realised he was hungry and was sure, from what he could see and smell, that the food would be good.

The gong sounded again twice more and about a dozen people arrived in the room. There were nods as people's paths crossed. Chloe briefly hugged a woman and two of the men. The chairs had been drawn back towards the walls, leaving a considerable space which the dozen or so now filled. Chloe kept hold of Andrew's hand and then Michael himself appeared, something which generated a muted but recognisable murmur of greeting from the others. Michael stood and held out his hands either side of him. Two others stood with him, one on his right one to his left, holding his hands. The rest then latched on, forming a rough circle. Chloe moved Andrew dexterously into place and, standing to his right, held his right hand. Another girl moved up to Andrew's left and took that hand. Within 10 seconds a rough circle of hands had formed.

Andrew had no idea what to expect, so he kept his eyes open though he could quickly see that most people were standing with eyes closed. Michael lifted and then lowered his left hand, saying as he finished *"the circle"*. The girl next to him had had her right arm raised and lowered; she now did the same with her left arm, again saying *"the circle"*. It took perhaps 10 seconds more for this odd little Mexican wave to complete. When it returned to Michael, he lifted both arms, still holding hands and said *"Widen the circle"*. Again this was copied by the girl on his left; and, of course, by the time this element of the Mexican wave had completed itself, all 12 people were standing, hands clasped with their arms in the air. Michael then said, in a way that even Andrew could see was meant to be the termination of 'prayers' (which was obviously what this was). *"We are the circle. Let us enjoy good food, company and widen the circle."*

With this, all eyes opened. Roughly half the people present went to start the process of finding a plate and helping themselves, the others – Chloe leading Andrew – went and sat to await their turn. Now Andrew had taken the scene in, he spotted a couple of Sisters standing quietly by the tables in case anyone needed help or advice. He also registered a couple of wine bottles and a range of beers on one of the tables. When Chloe took Andrew up to find a plate, Andrew made sure to return to his seat clutching a sizeable glass of red wine.

The food was varied and, Andrew had to admit,

excellent. The Angels certainly didn't stint on the essentials. Andrew sat in a chair next to Chloe and was about to say something to her when it became apparent that this was not what was done during meals. Instead, one of the Sisters had moved to a lectern and began reading aloud in a voice obviously meant to blot out any conversation.

From his Catholic background, Andrew quickly realised, with her first words *"Blessed are the poor in spirit for theirs is the Kingdom of Heaven"* that she was reading a version of the Sermon on the Mount. Jesus' summary – Andrew thought- in Matthew's Gospel. Over the next 10 minutes or so, the woman ran through all eight (Andrew now remembered) of the Blessings in the Sermon, offering a short commentary on what each meant for an Angel. Later, thinking back, Andrew realised that two pieces of dialogue had stuck in his mind. First, *"Blessed are the meek for they shall inherit the earth"*. Second *"Blessed are the peacemakers for they will be called children of God."* Andrew no longer had any active Christian faith. But these words had always appealed to him, even as a child, once he was old enough to know a little about the cruelties and peculiarities of the world. In a strange way, it was how he thought of his 'hidden role' for the Colonel – as a peace keeper.

The Sister read slowly, pausing on each of the eight beatitudes and the short explanation or commentary that followed that statement. People ate as they listened, and several – Andrew included – rose and refilled their plate as the reading continued. Well, thought Andrew, if the Colonel feels these people are dangerous revolutionaries, perhaps this will reassure him. But Andrew immediately realised the falsity of that argument; the early Christians' policies had been totally subversive of the social order in which they had found themselves in the Roman Empire. Such mild and 'reasonable' policies could, he realised, be equally subversive here and now.

Two other Sisters moved quietly around the room, clearing plates and the food remaining. Michael watched them and then spoke for the first time as they neared the end of the task. *"We had better move onto the real meat of the evening before everyone starts to relax after a hard week and doze off. I'm going to go round now and briefly introduce each of you. Most of you know many of the others present. But that's certainly not true for one of you, who will be new to almost everyone; and my guess is that some of the specialists we have here may not have met all their colleagues either."*

Michael started with Andrew saying merely *"Let me start with Andrew Davies, who has only just joined our organisation and who is here primarily to learn what we are about."* As Michael went round the room, introducing the others, Andrew realised that he was facing quite a battery of the Angel 'senior management' – he didn't know what else to call it. There were four members of the High Council apart from Michael – including the two most senior, the Muslim Jibril and Michael's number 2, Gabby. Of the other three men, one was an Afro-Caribbean who was introduced as 'head of the policy unit', one was Gabby's own number 2 in the finance area and the third was Ariel who (Andrew recalled from Freddy's briefing) spoke for environmental matters. Of the women, one turned out to be Sammy – the woman (into middle age Andrew thought) whom Freddy had described as the 'agony aunt but one tough lady'. The other two came, so far as Andrew could understand, from the personnel side and from some kind of policy co-ordination unit. Plus, of course, Chloe who was introduced by Michael briefly but fondly as *"known to you all, one of the first Angels on the scene; she's here – with Andrew – to keep our feet firmly on the ground."*

Michael promised that this first session would last no more than an hour. It was, he said, intended to chart the course for the rest of the weekend; and they would come back to three key topics for in-depth discussion later. *"Those three topics"* said Michael. *"First, the core of the Manifesto we shall have to put to the Electorate, to get them comfortable with the idea that voting for us is not voting for some La La Land version of reality. Second how are we going to use the Foundation – and its money – to the best advantage in this next 14 months? Third, how to use our technology to maximise our impact, specifically on the Millennial and Z generations? That should be more than enough for one weekend. If there is any time left over, we should home in on pre-Election strategies to get us known to our public. We need to get voters thinking of people like Gabby and Ariel here as people they'd like to know, normal decent citizens, with some good ideas for rescuing the country from its current crazy state."*

Andrew didn't try too hard to keep up with the next hour's debate. The people who were going to lead on the three topics outlined briefly how they would proceed when their 'turn' came later in the weekend. A couple of people indicated that they had very specific issues to put to Michael, who duly promised he would be available as needed. And that was it. By 9.30, the debate had not only ended but the participants had taken themselves off to sleep. Andrew himself, once back in his room, picked out a historical novel from the bookcase there, read one chapter, and fell quickly into what turned out to be a deep and dreamless sleep.

10

Andrew slept well and was awakened only by a bell that, according to his watch, meant it was 8am. He took a quick shower in his en-suite and headed downstairs. Breakfast, it turned out, was a more relaxed meal than dinner had been. He arrived when perhaps half the weekend's participants had appeared, quickly found where the cooked food was and enjoyed a good fry-up at a large table. His liking for fry-ups was a relic from his Army days and had never left him.

At this meal, people did talk to each other – there was no reading. Andrew nodded at the people sitting either side of him, both of whom promptly introduced themselves. One, a girl, Eva, was the HR expert he had seen last night, tall, handsome, slightly Slavic look he thought. The other was Ariel who, whatever his environmental views, clearly didn't feel the need to avoid eating meat.

The conversation was fairly inconsequential, though the girl at least showed interest in finding out a bit more about Andrew. He just enjoyed the food and some excellent coffee and responded to her questions politely but not very fully. When she talked about herself, it turned out that she had been an Angel for several years and had started working full-time for them about a year ago, as Michael had then started to ramp up operations ahead of the upcoming Election. In conversation, Eva made the same point that Michael had made last night. *"We don't see nearly enough new faces like yours – or at least not with skills like yours. I pulled up your entry on our data base last night – always good to know who you're spending time with. Impressive, I must say."* She smiled at him and turned to Ariel.

Chloe arrived towards the end of Andrew's meal. Her idea of breakfast was clearly 2 cups of coffee, 1 slice of toast – and no conversation! Of Michael there was no sign and when Andrew mentioned this fact Eva smiled at him. *"Michael gets lobbied mercilessly at weekends like this. Someone will be in there with him, trying to get extra funding for some personal brainwave. It's just as well that Michael always seems to have money available to meet the more sensible ideas; and he has a charming way of saying 'no' when the ideas aren't sensible or don't fit his strategy."*

Another bell sounded. Eva looked at her watch. *"10 minutes to kick-off. It looks a lovely day again out there – my morning run was really good today. Michael will try to ensure that we get at least several hours free after lunch. He's a great believer in the value of fresh air – and, thank God, in the diminishing value of lengthy meetings."*

The policy session turned out to be in a room that Andrew had not so far seen. The room was dominated by a rectangular and very substantial table with – he counted – 14 chairs set around. Depressingly familiar large screens sat at each end of the table. And each place at the table was equipped with an A4-sized pad and several cheap pens. At one end, a smaller table offered water, glasses and what Andrew called 'nibbles'.

All those attending walked in within a couple of minutes of each other. Andrew made sure he sat next to Chloe and on the same side as he thought Michael would sit; a chair in the centre of one side of the table, without in any way appearing to be different, looked as though it had been set out as Michael's.

When Michael himself walked in, there was a collective muted welcome from the others as there had been the previous evening. Michael sat where Andrew had expected, allowed people about 20 seconds to get settled, and kicked off. *"Those of you who have been here before know what to expect. It's 9.30 now. We will finish by 12.30. Everyone is welcome to come and go as they wish. Drinks – which will include fresh coffee – are at the end there. One person – for our first session me I'm afraid part of the time – will have the floor. But questions and interventions are very welcome at any time; and everyone must feel free to say exactly what they think. If you're critical, you are rubbishing an argument or idea not the person setting it out. And, remember, we don't have time to play the traditional British middle-class game of damning with faint praise. I don't want to hear things like 'that's quite* a good idea' or 'I rather like that'. The ideas we discuss today will be fleshed out and set out to the Electorate within months. 'So, are these policies broadly desirable? Do they make sense? Can people get enthusiastic about them? How do we make them enthusiastic?

Session 1 is central: what we're going to put to the Electorate, that enough of them will like and believe in: policies that will mark the Angels out as different from, and better than, the traditional parties."* The room darkened modestly and the screens came alive. Andrew noticed for the first time that a young Angel was sitting at the far corner of the room, controlling the equipment.

Michael went on. *"We have to appeal to the millions of decent, hard-working people in this country who are fed up. They are fed up with the rich not paying their share. They are fed up with people at the other end who sponge off the NHS and the benefits system. They are suspicious of immigrants unless these people have come here to work and do not represent a threat to their own jobs, housing and health resources. They are sick of unpunished scamming of their credit cards or bank accounts and what they see (probably not altogether accurately) as a large pool of under-reported and unsolved local crime. Those are the triggers in their minds that we have to pull.*

We have to reassure them that we care about all this, that we are nicer than the Tories and more sensible than Labour. We need to show we are willing and able to create a new social contract, though I'd never use that term in public- I doubt if one in 100 voters would understand what it meant. In which people contribute fairly but can also expect a proper safety net available to them if things go wrong. We need to show how our existing policies towards housing, young families and combatting addiction will work. We have to convince them that we have practical and successful policies to apply, as we currently do on a modest scale through our help stores, our addiction centres, and our financial advice. But we have to get them to believe that we can replicate the success at a national level if and when we get control over the huge resources the State already throws at these problems."

Michael paused for effect. *"And we have to do all that without frightening the materialistic set into thinking that we're just another form of Corbynism out to fleece them. There's a world of difference between fleecing the rich and making sure they don't use every tax dodge and tax haven in the book to avoid paying their share. And, if all of that wasn't enough, we have to do it while convincing them that our MPs will not just be another band of self-aggrandising self-satisfied people out to get what they can from the body politic. Personally, I think that will be one of the easier parts."*

Andrew did his best to keep up with the subsequent debate; he felt he owed it to the Colonel. Most of the talking in this first session was down to Michael and the Policy Section chief. The key element of what the Angels had in mind for taxes seemed to be a system with lower marginal rates (35% at the top) but with even the richest being forced to pay a tax rate of at least 30% on all their income, not just what they chose to keep in the UK and declare. Likewise, companies including the big US-based tech giants would have to pay at least 20% of profits. *"No more rotten apples"* as the Policy chief put it – the nearest thing to a joke in the whole morning. He spoke to a set of slides that showed just how much extra revenue could be gathered in by these means; and the meeting readily agreed that this was a great Election platform on which to fight. However, as the Policy man made clear, some of the tax benefits and loopholes that would have to go might well prove less digestible. Much he warned would depend on how seriously the other parties took the Angels before the Election – and therefore how much negative analysis they would throw at Angel proposals. Ideally, the Angels would get across the basic equity of their ideas and stay off too many specifics.

The second half of the morning was devoted to discussion of public spending, where Andrew quickly lost the thread. By lunch, he had written down only the argument that much would depend on the Angels showing how they could use existing State spending to better effect than now. As Michael put it at one point *"We should have no problem with some of the ideas this will involve – like doing away with winter fuel payments to those elderly people rich enough to be paying high marginal tax rates. But some of that is small beer in the wider scheme of things. We're going to have to be ultra-careful on things like how we propose to improve the NHS, the ultimate sacred cow for the Electorate here. There'll be a separate and long policy brief on this nearer the time – which I'm sure you will all pore over."*

Lunch came none too soon for Andrew, who had also by then decided that he would skip the afternoon session on electoral issues, although he had been assured it would be short. He justified this (which he found anyway an unbelievably boring subject) by convincing himself that he mustn't make it look like he was desperate to tag onto everything the Angels did. The decider for him was the weather which still looked beautiful and the news, from Chloe at lunch, that there was a nice 9-hole golf course reserved here for conference participants. Apparently the centre was often hired out for events which benefitted from such facilities.

Most of the others, Andrew realised, would go back after lunch; but they were here because they were full-time participants, he wasn't. *"Dinner will be at 7"* Chloe told him, when he informed her that he would skip the afternoon session. *"The swimming pool's nice too. I might be there myself around 5."* Andrew promised to look out for her.

Andrew then passed a very pleasant and easily organised afternoon. One of the Sisters insisted on taking him to the Pro-Shop (all of 5 minutes' walk). Clubs, suitable shoes and enough balls for even a relatively poor player like Andrew were readily available; and he enjoyed the ability to hack his way around the course on his own. He sometimes found the social side of golf a little trying, especially where the other players were highly competitive, as they typically were in the City – from which his opponents normally came.

By 5 he was at the pool-side, the sun still beating down enough to make one of the shadier areas there very welcome. There was no sign of Chloe. But several of the other Angels appeared, including Eva in a bathing costume that would not have been out of place in a beauty contest. Her hair was tied back, long black hair flowed down her back, a long and sinuous back. She was a little on the thin side he thought; but she looked good, her whole being seemed to radiate health and well-being. Andrew had always found this combination alluring and, here, it immediately made him think of Chloe.

Eva dived in and swam a dozen or so lengths competently and quickly. Andrew was in the shallow end and couldn't help but watch her with approval. Eventually, she stopped her swimming at his end, and stood up in the shallows. There was no-one else within yards of them.

"You chose wisely" she said. *"This afternoon wasn't the most interesting I've taken part in here. Michael has worked out that we need around 7 million votes at the Election; and, of course, these need to be concentrated in the 'right' places. Toby our psephologist had endless insights to offer. His people are clearly doing a vast amount of work at the Foundation to identify the couple of hundred seats we are most likely to be able to make a showing in. And, of course, Michael is very concerned to get everything as right as possible. But for those of us who just have faith, it was frankly pretty boring. What have you been doing?"*

Andrew explained his own activities that afternoon. Eva looked at him thoughtfully. *"I hope you don't like being on your own too much. Perhaps you and I could tag up at dinner and afterwards? Michael doesn't encourage too much sex at these events; but he isn't against it either. And I haven't had a real man for weeks now – just too busy."*

Andrew was a little taken aback by her frankness. But he quickly went on to think, as he had with Vy, that accepting the offer would be both enjoyable in its own right and could only help get him more readily accepted by the Angels. He'd been told to stay away from the Sisters; but Eva wasn't one of those. He certainly wasn't

Showroom Cinema

NTL: Dear Englan

Date: Mon 29 Jan 2024   Time: 12:00

Screen 3

Row: D   Seat: 14

Members   Price: 15.00

2605310/1 BOXTILL101 Max Barker 29/01/24 11:51 Card

To Book Tickets Online Visit
www.showroomworkstation.org.uk

likely to get what he really wanted, which was Chloe in suitably amorous mood. *"I'd really enjoy that"* he said. *"I just hope I don't disappoint."* *"Not much chance of that, I think"* Eva said in reply and had the grace to look mildly embarrassed. *"Remember, I downloaded your CV and, of course, Vy's write up went with it. If you could download mine, by the way, I equally don't think you'd be disappointed. Though it would stress that I really go for men who are both forceful and gentle – and"* she added with a slight smile *"I like to be on top."*

With that, she turned in the water and began swimming lengths again, vigorously. Andrew again cursed Vy and her 'write-up'; but at least, as he got out of the pool, he did accept that his time with Vy had had consequential benefits.

Supper at 7 turned out to be good (again) and wholly informal. Andrew saw that several of the Angels had paired off and were talking to each other as though no-one else were present. Andrew had an undoubted spasm of jealousy when he saw that one of the couples was Chloe with Ariel. Now Andrew knew why he had instinctively disliked the man.

Eva left him alone until the end of the meal and then quite openly walked across to him and said, in tones that anyone nearby would hear, *"Give me 10 minutes. I'm in Room 11."* Andrew duly waited, about 20 minutes he thought would send the right signal; and he enjoyed another glass of the Shiraz available. He then walked up the stairs to Room 11, knocked quietly and went in without waiting for an invitation. Eva was standing by the mirror, in a short and thin nightdress. *"Make yourself at home"* she said, getting into bed without further delay or any form of foreplay. *"You'll find condoms in the drawer – Michael is always so paranoid about that that I suspect the Sisters carry them 24/7 – just in case. By the way, if no-one has told you, never try and have unprotected sex with an Angel. That's strictly reserved for only the most serious relationships – when you've chosen a partner for life."*

Andrew quickly stripped off and got into bed beside Eva. 'Strong but gentle' he kept thinking to himself; but in reality Eva was on him (quite literally on top of him) within two minutes; and, for the rest of the evening, Andrew had more on his hands than trying to stick to a mantra.

11

ndrew awoke just before the first bell would anyway have roused him. He rolled over. Eva was nowhere to be seen but he quickly found a short message on her side of the bed. *Have gone for my run. CU at breakfast.*

Andrew rose and slipped out of the door to his own room. He showered, shaved and dressed leisurely and informally, noting that the weather was still set fair. Breakfast was in full swing by the time he had arrived, with no sign of Eva or Chloe. As before, he ate well but, this time, alone.

Towards the end of the meal, Michael made a brief appearance. *"I only want the die-hards at this morning's session. We're going to be looking at how we develop our local Election candidates and give them a public presence that will reassure people to vote for them. Vital work but probably only for half of you here. Lunch will be at 12.30 sharp. I would appreciate everyone being here for that as I want to send you all out with a very clear message to think over in the coming weeks."* With that, he was gone; and, over the next 10 minutes about half of those present drifted out, fairly obviously to attend the rest of the session. The rest stayed on, using their mobiles and rarely talking. Gabby's deputy was sprawled on a chair next to him and Andrew did exchange a few pleasantries with him. The man opened by excusing his continued presence there *"No point in my going to this. Michael and the others will have worked out how much their policies are likely to cost; and it's people like me who have to find the right amount of money at the right time. Fortunately, at present that's not an issue. I just hope I can say that in a year's time."*

Andrew spent the rest of the morning drinking good coffee and wandering lazily round the attractive and surprisingly large grounds. Eva was still nowhere in sight; he presumed she had gone straight from her run to the morning session.

At 12.30 sharp, the bell rang and Andrew again found himself in the main dining room. Eva was there but, apart from a brief hug and kiss from her, she made no allusion at all to the previous night. Andrew wondered idly whether she had completed her review yet of his performance, which he guessed was bound to follow at some point in the near future. Chloe was there too, smiled sweetly at him and said *"I believe Michael wants to see you straight after lunch. When you've done, come and find me; I'll drive you back to London. We all get the afternoon off*

72

for good behaviour." Chloe then smiled to herself, as this simple statement had clearly stirred some memory.

Michael was present at the meal but didn't seem to be eating. Indeed, Andrew didn't recall having seen him eat anything since the first meal on Friday night. Michael allowed a few minutes to pass and then spoke without introduction but in a voice that immediately cut through and silenced the few conversations around the room. *"This is probably the last time any of us will have a relaxed and pleasant weekend like this. Until the Election is over in 13 months and 27 days. Even then, if things go to plan, most of you will still be wondering when you are ever going to draw breath and have some 'me-time'. I apologise now. But we are about to move a mountain and that doesn't happen without the blood, sweat and tears of a lot of labourers. And the fact is, that while we have a growing number of labourers, you are special, which is why you are here. On the inside, doing the heavy lifting.*

*Those of you with a Christian education should also reflect on Jesus' parable of the workers in the vineyard. Whether these people arrived at the beginning of the day or near the end, he had all of them paid the same rate – no hourly Minimum Wage obviously. But the point he was making is one you have to take to heart now. We need to add thousands of workers in the coming months. I hope many of them will do it for love; but people also have to live and so we will be paying many of them. And, at the end of it, if we succeed they will feel just as much part of that success as you do, though you – not them – will have done the heavy lifting. It's just something we have to live with and not be precious about the fact that we were here first. **I** will know what each of you has done. I hope and pray that will be enough for you, plus the satisfaction of an amazing job. Now, go back to* *your bases and gear up for what will be one of the great fights of the 21st Century. You are here, we together will make history. The circle can't be expanded enough without you."*

With that Michael left. And the others, after a momentary silence, started to gather up their things to leave too. A Sister appeared silently at Andrew's side. She said quietly *"Michael would like to see you now; I'll take you to him."*

She led him out of the room and to a small room a few steps away. As when Andrew had first seen him, Michael was standing and he turned as Andrew entered. *"I hope you've enjoyed the weekend"* Michael said, extending an arm to indicate several chairs that Andrew could choose from. They sat.

Michael went on. *"I've just been talking about how little time we have so I won't waste any of yours. We hardly know each other yet. But I sense in you someone who could be a seriously important part of our team. You finding Chloe was serendipity that we mustn't waste. What I (and you too) have to do now is to find ways of accelerating the mutual 'get-to-know you' process. To see whether you really have the qualities I can sense – and whether you want to use them for the Angels' benefit.*

What you need to see is the reality behind this movement – in particular, what 'hard lifting' can actually mean. Yes, we try to keep to higher principles than the other political parties and that isn't difficult most of the time. But the world's an unpleasant place full of some very dangerous opponents. So the Angels can't just be fluffy do-gooders. At least a few of us have to be prepared to get our hands dirty if it's really necessary. Are you willing to be one of those is a key question for you? Are you as good as I think you are? That's the key question for me.

74

Andrew didn't know quite what to say. But he sensed that some kind of important offer was being made to him. It sounded, at first sight, as though he had hit the jackpot, in getting the Angels to chase him rather than him having to chase them. Andrew chose his reply with care. *"The Army and business life have both taught me a lot, so I think I understand your drift. What exactly are you suggesting?"*

Michael took a few seconds to reply. *"Chloe can be what you would probably have called in your Army days your handler. What I'm suggesting is that over the next few weeks – and it will have to be quick, we don't have the time for anything else – she will suggest a small number of 'tasks' for you. These will all be tasks that could raise moral or other issues with you. You will have to decide if the ends justify the means and whether you are prepared to do them; then, if you are, execute them. At the end of each task, I will make sure that you get the chance to see first-hand one of the key parts of our operation and talk to whoever you like there. At the end of that process, you and I agree whether you should be 'out' or 'in'; but on a much better basis of mutual understanding than we could possibly have now.*

There is danger in this for the Angels. If you decide not to join us, you will have seen something of our less attractive underbelly and could use that against us. We shall just have to limit the risk of that as far as possible, hence for example having Chloe as your handler – Chloe who to almost everyone is really a small cog in the Angel world. But, if I'm right in what I sense in you, the prize for us – a highly-competent able operative who is right there on the inside – and someone who understands and has what we really need – makes it worth our taking the risk."

Andrew thought he had better lighten the atmosphere a little. *"I did have – 'enjoy' would be too strong a word – a classical education. What you're describing sounds a bit like a potted version of the Labours of Hercules. Though I would stress I haven't started by killing my wife and child, like Hercules did, and it's obvious you have something like 12 weeks in mind, rather than the 12 years I think Hercules worked for his 'handler'. Also, if I remember correctly, most of his labours involved catching dangerous animals or stealing things that had magical powers. I am presuming that what you want is rather more down to earth."*

"Yes, indeed" replied Michael and stood up, indicating clearly that the meeting was over. *"I hope Chloe's company will help alleviate any strain you may experience from what I've suggested. Trust her fully. I do."* Three seconds later, he was gone. Twenty seconds later. Andrew was outside looking for Chloe and his ride back to London.

12

Andrew and Chloe didn't say much as she drove them back to London. She seemed on a high, singing quietly to herself at one point. Andrew, for his part, turned over in his mind what Michael had said. Yes, surely the Colonel would be pleased that Andrew had been so quickly accepted by the Angels. But what actually was he going to be asked to do? And, if it were illegal – which Andrew rather suspected was possible – would the Colonel's powers protect Andrew if things went wrong?

By the time they got back to London and Chloe was ready to drop him off, Andrew at least had established that, as of now, Chloe had no idea of the role she would be playing as his handler; and Andrew admitted to himself that she could handle him as much as she liked.

Chloe offered a cheek for a perfunctory kiss as he got out of the car. *"I'll be in touch in a couple of days"* she said. *"Be good."*

Andrew used the next couple of days to make sure his visitors from the Middle East were being gainfully employed and starting to understand what 'Know Your Customer' – KYC to those in the anti-money laundering business – meant in real-life cases. *"Just remember"* Andrew later recalled himself saying. *"A banker with a rich new customer has a fine line to walk. He needs to ask questions about the source of the money and its likely uses; but to do so in a way that is not going to alienate a client who can probably see no reason on earth why his bank should be poking its nose into his business. And you have to be able to write it all up, so that your regulator – and any international team from the Financial Action Task Force – can be satisfied you have done your due diligence. Not an easy balance to strike; rich men tend to find it easy to find another bank if they get fed up with you."* When Andrew thought about it, he realised that he was having to find a similar balance with the Angels.

It was actually not until Wednesday that Chloe got in touch, to suggest an 'Angel evening' on Thursday night – *"Good food, drink and dancing – with a promise to get you home by midnight so you can work on Friday if you have to."* Andrew pressed Chloe to check that she herself would be there. *"Yes, with Hazel and a few others too"* was the answer. Then she added *"By the way, Michael has asked me to raise something with you. He says I'll have all the details by tomorrow and he says you know about it. Is that right?"* *"Well"* replied Andrew *"I certainly know something was on the way; but, as to what it is, I have no more idea than you.*" And that's how they left it, though Chloe did say she would be round at his flat half an hour or so early, so that she could explain whatever it was that Michael wanted.

By Wednesday afternoon, Andrew had been in touch with the Colonel and arranged a short meeting at one of the safe houses, in the rather upmarket tailor that Andrew liked to frequent. Andrew felt that now was the time to start, if he were going to do something about the colour of most of his wardrobe to fit in with the Angels; so it was a case of two birds with one stone.

Andrew arrived at the shop around 5 p.m. as agreed and thinking, rightly, that there wouldn't be many other customers around. The shop had several fitting rooms at the back, one of which Andrew knew from past experience was much bigger than such a room would ever normally be and soundproofed. He selected a range of the tailor's own brand of shirts, and took the armful of brightly coloured shirts with him to the room. Where, not surprisingly, the Colonel was sitting and looking like he had been there some time, although no sherry was in sight.

Andrew quickly reported his actions to date, making sure he covered in detail only the parts of Michael's weekend seminar that he thought would interest the Colonel. Andrew explained the proposed 'labours of Hercules'; and sat back to await the Colonel's reply. *"You've done well, Andrew, remarkably well in the time available. All I can suggest is that you tackle the first labour as soon as you can. The bits of the empire that I suggest you ask to 'inspect', as part of the deal after you've done each 'labour', are the money side of the Foundation itself, the policy section you describe and Michael's own personal household. It might be very useful later to know who is who in the group around him, and who really matters. As for what you say about the current expansion of activity and the focus on next year's Election, I can't say any of that comes as a great surprise. But your report does bear out a lot of what I've been hearing from other sources. As I say, well done. Let's keep in touch.*

By the way, I guess you may want to have a get-out if one of these labours goes horribly wrong and you attract the attention of our wonderful police. Do you remember the 'get out of jail' phone number you memorised last time?" Andrew confirmed that he did and repeated it to satisfy the Colonel. *"If you are arrested, just make sure that is the one phone call you are allowed to make. And do please try to make sure that you aren't being held for GBH or, worse, murder. So much more paperwork and legwork for us in those circumstances."*

With that, the Colonel left. Andrew spent a further 30 minutes choosing half a dozen new shirts, designed to co-ordinate with his Angel bands and, if he were honest, to show off his well-toned figure and healthy complexion. Then he returned home and, aware that he had skimped on the gym-work recently, spent a couple of hours in the neighbouring gym, following that with a leisurely swim and steam room visit.

Thursday evening came quickly enough. Chloe had warned him not to wear too much – *"The dance floor gets as hot as hell even when it isn't 30C or more outside like now."* He put his 3 bands on, and was slightly surprised to find that he had actually felt underdressed until he had done it. He mixed up a jug of pina colada, to go with the continuing good weather, hoping that would appeal to Chloe.

When she arrived, it turned out that pina colada would do her very well; and the first 20 minutes of her visit saw her down two large glasses *(we're not driving anywhere tonight")* and reminisce about the weekend which she had obviously enjoyed. *"Isn't Michael great?"* she asked, clearly without expecting a reply. *"I just love weekends like that. They make me feel pumped up and ready to cope with anything."* She paused. *"Well, now, I'd better pass on what Michael said before the drink makes me forget or not care."*

She sat and seemed to collect her thoughts. *"This is what Michael told me to say. One of the big challenges we face is getting increasing amounts of air-time as the Election approaches, given that our political rivals control most of the media. And it has to be good, positive, news – getting people to start thinking there is a steady swing of opinion towards the idea that a government of Angels would be a breath of fresh air. And that it can't be worse than what we're lumbered with now.*

So far, so good. But what he then said was that we can get a lot of this organised in advance, for example by a steady stream of well-known people coming out and saying that they are 'for us'. We need particularly to influence younger people. But there will also be value in getting people more generally to come off the fence, especially if they come from non-political walks of life. He talked for example about getting endorsements from people in organisations like The National Trust, The Mothers' Union and I can't remember what else. People – he said – who would not be known to the general public but who could really resonate with a lot of voters. He said the NT has 5 million members which sounds extraordinary, so I may have got that wrong."

"I get the idea" replied Andrew *"but what has that got to do with me?"* Chloe looked at him. *"All I can tell you is what he said. In some areas, we've got volunteers lined up, to come out for us when the time is ripe. In others, we are going to need to have a few people whose hand is forced. He wants me to introduce you to an Angel called Mark tonight. Mark is going to ask you to help him pin down someone who we need – I think he's a big footballer – but who isn't going to do it unless he's pressured to do it. Michael said it would be good for you and that you'd be a good persuader if necessary. Anyway, let's go – it's a very 'in' club in the West End – and I'll introduce you to Mark. He can take it from there. As you probably guessed, the manager of the club is one of us; and, because Michael says it's work, the Angels will be footing what is bound to be a big bill, even with Angel discounts."* That was all Chloe would or could say. Andrew went off to cast a final eye over himself in the mirror; Chloe went to the loo. They left, quickly found a taxi and about 30 minutes later pulled up in one of the parts of Mayfair that Andrew knew was normally quite out of his league.

Not for the first time, Andrew was struck by how much easier and nicer it was to get into a building with a pretty girl on your arm. Chloe anyway seemed to know the main bouncer on the door; they were in and headed for the bar (Andrew guessed it was just the first of several) within a minute. Chloe looked at him – Andrew thought a little pensively – and said *"I haven't been fully honest with you. I'm going to dance now"* she waved in the general direction of the back of the building from which dance music was wafting. *"Mark is over there. I'll bring him over."*

Mark turned out to be short, rather thick-set and about 35. Chloe introduced them and they shook hands. *"Come and find me later"* Chloe said to Andrew and, without further ado, left them. Mark looked speculatively at Andrew. He ordered two club martinis without asking Andrew what he wanted and then gestured to a recessed area to the right of the bar, where there were several substantial leather chairs. He said *"There aren't too many members in yet, which is good. Michael says I should not hide anything from you, so here's how it looks to me.*

There's a footballer due in here later. One of the England team, you'll recognise him. One of the Angel girls, who has 'befriended' him, has been told to make sure he's here by 10. She'll then leave him to our tender mercies. Your mission, should you accept it – wonderful how old telly gives you things to say – is to help me persuade him that, in about 6 months, he's going to come out with a public statement endorsing the Angels. That's all we have to do; that's all he has to agree to. If we succeed, there'll only be another 20 on my list to do the same with. You get to do just this one."

"Fine" Andrew replied. *"But what miracle ingredient do you have with you to get him to agree, let alone stick to an agreement that is some months ahead? Or is this girl he's with so pretty that he'll go along with you just to keep her? I've always thought these guys have the choice of almost any woman they want."*

Mark said nothing, just reached into his left trouser pocket and handed over a small mobile phone. *"This is what we'll be showing him before we ask nicely"* Mark said.

Probably best if you just watch like he will. There are two short feature films." Mark pressed a couple of buttons and handed the phone over. It was dark enough in this part of the bar for Andrew to be able to see clearly. There was a soundtrack but it was low and Andrew could feel fairly safe that no-one was near enough to overhear it.

Both short films featured the footballer who, though Andrew was not a football fan, even he recognised. The first seemed to have been taken in a room, perhaps in the footballer's own pad. There were just 2 people, the footballer and a man who turned out to be his tax adviser. Tax, of course, was an area where Andrew thought he knew a fair amount, given its role in money-laundering. And he needed only one run of the film to see what it meant. The footballer was using a tax loophole, seemingly through a Cayman-incorporated vehicle, to avoid tax on a significant part of his income. The dodge – quite common to Andrew's knowledge – was to get sponsors for boots, other kit, and TV endorsement ads featuring the footballer, to pay money direct to his Cayman bank account. That meant the money would not appear then on any UK tax return, although the work would have been done in the UK; and, if the guy was clever **and** dishonest, it would never appear on a UK form at all. That left just Cayman income tax which of course was zero. About £5 million a year seemed to be at stake. But, or so Andrew thought, the dodge **was** just about legal. So why would the footballer worry?

The subject of the second feature was much clearer. It looked like it had been shot in poor light, somewhere tucked well away. Again two people, this time the footballer and an Asiatic who was very obviously the representative of a gambling circle who had 'bought' the footballer's co-operation to 'influence' the outcome of games. The footballer had clearly failed to deliver on at least one of his commitments; and, in the face of some pretty open threats, was offering to pull some more strings in future games, for 'less than the usual'. The quality of the shots left something to be desired. But, Andrew judged, any football fan who saw it would have exploded in rage. The footballer was bent, it was clear.

Andrew handed the phone back. *"So, this is blackmail?"* Andrew asked. *"You could call it that"* Mark replied. *"But it's hard to have any sympathy for a sleaze-bag like this guy. I really feel for the girl who has had to put up with him for the last few weeks, to set up the cameras and get the results. That is Angel duty above and beyond! Even though she was helped by the great range of miniature drones that someone in the movement has developed. From now on, anyone should be working on the basis that, when you say 'I'd like to be a fly on the wall', you probably can be; that is exactly what these drones look like. "*

Andrew downed half his martini, though that wasn't one of his usual tipples, and reflected. *"I'll do most of the work"* said Mark. *"You just have to sit there, follow up my points if you think it's necessary, and make sure we stay undisturbed."*

Shortly after, the footballer arrived, with a stunning tall blonde on his arm. She had obviously been primed as to what was happening, because she immediately located Mark sitting in the corner with Andrew. *"Jimmy"* she whispered to the footballer *"this is the man I told you I wanted you to meet. I'll fix some of your usual champagne from*

the bar and then go and powder my nose. We can dance later."
Andrew had taken an immediate dislike to Jimmy; he
was dressed in an expensive suit that still somehow said
'barrow boy' about its wearer. And the man clearly had
huge ego problems which, for example, meant it took
him a few seconds now to focus on Mark and say, without
enthusiasm *"OK girl, Just 5 minutes."* Jimmy slapped the
girl's backside familiarly; and Andrew disliked him still
more. The girl's expression slipped for just a second – a
brief malevolent glance at Jimmy. Then, she recovered
her poise, moved over, spoke quietly to the barman
and disappeared. The barman appeared with a glass of
champagne for Jimmy, in less than 20 seconds – the
bottle had obviously been standing ready to be poured.
Jimmy took it without thanks and threw himself down
next to Mark.

*"I promised Jenny I'd give you 5 minutes; and I hope she's
already made it clear I don't do charity signatures, team shirts or
any of that crap. You'll have to see my agent if you want those
– and pay the going rate."* Mark smiled, a little sourly in
reply. *"Now that's one thing I don't have – a picture of you
with your agent. Though I do have a couple of short videos with
other people you know. We'll have to make do with those."*
Mark pushed a button on his phone, which he had left
lying on the table and handed it to Jimmy.

Andrew, reflecting later, realised that he had really
enjoyed the next 10 minutes. Jimmy had watched the
first of the two short videos without comment and with
his face recording only a hardening around the mouth
and a short grimace of distaste. Jimmy had only got a few
seconds into the second video before he started as though

to rise and swore quickly under his breath. Presumably, in the desire to see just how far the video went, Jimmy relapsed back into his suit and watched the rest, his facial expressions alternating between anger and fear.

"Jeez" was all Jimmy could say initially when the video finished. He looked around him at the room and then said in a low urgent voice to Mark. *"Let's talk somewhere a bit more private."* Jimmy rose and, having had a quick word with the barman – Jimmy was obviously a regular here. He led them through a door on the other side of the bar which led down a short dimly-lit corridor and then into what were obviously small bedrooms on one side. Jimmy took one of the rooms that had an open door, looked inside and then said *"This'll do. Now, who the hell are you two and what do you want? Journalists by the look of you."*

Mark smiled briefly. *"No, we're not journalists though we do know plenty of them who will be eating out of our hands for a lifetime if we give them a scoop like this. No, we're friends of Jenny who, by the way in case you are in any doubt, will have left by the time you get out of here; and she won't be calling you again. We are people who –probably quite foolishly – are prepared to sit on these videos –and eventually hand every copy back to you – in return for just one simple thing."*

"Those tapes are fakes" spluttered Jimmy. *"No-one will believe you. And, anyway, the first one doesn't even show anything illegal – if it weren't a fake, that is."*

Mark smiled quietly again. *"The one thing you are right about is that the legality of what's covered by the first tape is in debate. Though I doubt if your chances of captaining England would last long after its publication. And it might anyway make some of your sponsors think again. But we were thinking we would start with the second tape where there is no doubt about the illegality involved. As for whether it's real or not, just think about the backing documents we might have to prove its accuracy. Like an affidavit from the Asian gentleman who was with you – that he reluctantly but legally provided in return for our allowing him to get out of England. Jenny might reappear too and talk about some of your other little foibles – like the party drugs you supply to some of your more favoured visitors.*

No, I think we can safely say your career will go downhill rapidly as soon as publication happens. And all you have to do, to avoid that – we're not after your money – is to stand up one day, in a few months when we tell you, in a Press Conference. And all you have to do then is to announce to the world (and your 300,000 social media followers) that you have been looking into the Angels' plans for the future; and that, you Jimmy, will be voting for the Angels at the coming Election. We'll write your little speech for you. You won't even have to go and vote when the time comes. Your announcement will be a 3 day wonder and then the press caravan will move on, having had the effect we need.

Tell you what. Keep the videos with our compliments – we have more copies of course. Think things through quietly and then call the number that's at the end of the video and tell us your answer. If it's 'yes' then just sit back and wait until we are ready to go live with your 'coming out' for the Angels. If it's 'no' just count down the hours you will have left before the shit-storm hits you."

Andrew hadn't said anything during this conversation. Now, to his surprise, he found himself rising to his feet and looking down at Jimmy. *"Personally,*

Andrew said *"I rather hope you say 'no'. People like you sicken me."* With that, Andrew and Mark left and returned to the bar, leaving the footballer holding the mobile phone disconsolately in his hand.

From Andrew's point of view, the evening tailed off pretty quickly. He found Chloe and danced a bit with her and with Hazel. But his mind was whirring over the earlier events and he realised that he was – and would remain – poor company. Chloe seemed to sense this; and by 11 she had said to him *"You've had enough, I'll get you home"*.

They sat, silently, in the taxi. When they arrived, Chloe declined an invitation to come into his flat. But Andrew did insist on talking with her in the street for a couple of minutes. *"You can tell Michael"* said Andrew *"that the first labour is completed. What I now want him to do is to set up a meeting for me with someone senior who can tell me all about the money side of the Angels. He'll understand I think."*

And Andrew, by midnight as promised, found himself sitting up in his bed and pondering the night's events. What Michael had managed to do, he realised, was to expose one aspect of Angel business that Andrew could hardly condone but which – Andrew could see – made a lot of sense, if the ultimate aim was for the Angels to take power. Also, Andrew felt strongly, if such tactics had to be employed, people like Jimmy deserved that – and a whole lot worse. At least, Andrew reflected, he hadn't been actively involved in anything that could be called illegal – if you ignored the blackmail angle.

13

It took Andrew nearly a week to get the 'reward' he wanted for the first 'labour'. Two days after he had left Chloe on the street, he took a call from a man who introduced himself as Mo – *"Most people can't spell Mohammed in any of its forms"* the man said cheerfully. *"I understand you want to talk about Angel finances and I'm your man for that. Where would you like to meet up and when?"* Andrew knew what he wanted. *"I'll come to you wherever that is; I want to see the financial heart of this empire. And, believe me, I shall have a lot of questions – both about where the money comes from and where it goes."*

"Well" replied Mo. *"That makes a nice change. I nearly always have to come up to London to see the money boys. If you're serious about coming here, you need to get to Northampton – I'll email you the address and directions. Shall we say around*

10, perhaps next Wednesday?" Andrew's diary, of course, was blank and, after failing to get Mo to bring the day forward, he agreed. Mo rang off, saying helpfully. *"We have parking here, if you drive."*

Chloe kept away in the next couple of days. Andrew filled his time with gym work, a little shopping and a day's visit to his aunt down in Guildford. He didn't feel particularly close to her and, in fact, they had remarkably little in common. But, when his parents had died, Andrew had promised himself that he would always keep in touch with her, as often as his Army duties and, later, his work commitments allowed. He wanted to have at least a few anchors in the 'real' world.

On the Wednesday, Andrew drove through North London early, though that still meant doing only about 19 miles in the first hour. Around 8.30 he pulled into the service station just south of Northampton on the M1 and enjoyed – well, perhaps that was too strong a word – 'took' an English breakfast with extra toast and coffee. Just after 10, he found The Foundation office he had been given directions to, though he drove past it the first time round, it was so small and unobtrusive; on a small industrial estate mostly given over to small company warehousing and retail outlets. The parking was directly outside the building. Andrew parked and went in.

There was no Receptionist. Instead, a phone and a message saying 'Please buzz if you need us', which Andrew duly did. About 30 seconds later, a smart but casually dressed man pushed open the door opposite the phone. The man – short, slim and bespectacled, maybe 40 – walked out. *"Hello"* he said cheerfully. *"I'm Mo. You must be Andrew. Come in and make yourself at home. Would you like some coffee, though I warn you now it's not brilliant?"* Andrew declined politely and they went through into a small open area with 5 or 6 rooms or offices running off it. There was a single table and a handful of supposedly easy chairs around, all of which looked like they had been bought in a job lot for perhaps £100 from a local clearance firm. Virtually nothing on the walls. The Angels certainly didn't go in for the luxury that Andrew now almost took for granted after his time in the City.

The office Mo led him into was similarly spartan, though perfectly functional. The one thing that looked expensive was the computer array on the desk. But, even here, there were none of the Reuters screens or any other components of a typical London dealing room to be seen. Whatever went on here did not involve money management or market activity on any scale.

Andrew looked round, slightly surprised and Mo, watching him, smiled. *"Yes, I'm sure this isn't what you had expected, Andrew. But I promise you that this one floor – there are 7 of us who work here – is not just the hub of The Foundation's money machine, it IS The Foundation's money machine."* Andrew, for his part, was prepared to listen but he found Mo's statement hard to believe.

"I think I'd better explain a bit" said Mo. *"The Angels have three basic sources of income. The first and primary source is from the dividends we get from the shareholding we have in Baldens, more on that in a minute. The second, quite modest, never more than 10%, is the revenue from the various clubs and activities we run. Trouble there, from a money point of view, is that Michael is much better at thinking up new social initiatives*

than he is at getting any money out of them. The third, and the only one for which we take any credit, is what one could call the 'exceptional items'. They are very few and far between. Again, more on that in a minute.

The point I want to emphasise though is that the money from Baldens requires no work or initiative from us – we just log the quarterly dividend payments. The second, the revenue flow, is primarily the responsibility of the Activities Division – all the grunt work and paper trail is done there. We just collect the net revenue in, if there is any and, from time to time, decide if the external auditors (who, of course, are London-based) need to conduct any checks for us or for the Charities Commission. Hardly labour-intensive for us.

The third source is, well, the result of very occasional and sizeable bets by us on markets. We've only done two of those in my 3 years here. The first was a long-running play we had on Bitcoin – bought before my time at around 20$ a time and sold early 2018 for thousands each. The second was when we built up a large long position in oil, when it fell to around $30 a barrel. We got out, about 18 months later at an average of about $65. Both of those operations basically required just two decisions by Michael, 1 to buy and 1 to sell. And the oil required action by the London firm we use for what little trading we do. Hence, this lean but not mean operation you see here.

To make it even simpler, our assets are held only in top quality safe form, mostly government bonds which we buy and hold, not trade. The nearest thing I have to a paper chase involving human involvement is the regular forecasting of our cash position. But, even here, Michael insists we hold £25 million in liquid form with the banks so that, even if we get things horribly wrong, there is a huge safety-net. If you don't have to profit-maximise, it's amazing what just a couple of people can do. Four of the seven of us here are competent in each of the areas we cover, providing back-up and incidentally checking on each other, seeing that everything is above board. We have no need to be registered with the financial regulators or anyone else. Hence we can manage with a tiny staff in a cheap, out of London, office – which is what you see."

Andrew thought for a moment. *"Let's talk about each of these separately. Tell me about Baldens first."* Mo came back immediately with a potted history he had obviously given many times before. *"The two Balden brothers began the supermarket business about 15 years ago. Michael I believe has known them for almost that long; but certainly, from near the outset, Michael supported their business. Even now, despite how big they've grown, you'd be amazed how much of the business that they see comes from Angels and their families. Almost at the beginning, while they were still a private company and in return for some much-needed finance, the brothers gave a 30% stake to the Angels, who at that time were hardly seen or known about. As the Balden business grew, so did our income; and, when the business went public, our shareholding became worth a good deal, a worth that we could cash in any time. They now make about £1.5 billion a year net profit from their 400 or so stores, and pay out 2/3rds of that in dividends. Michael decided about four years ago that we needed to reduce our holding because it was a case of just too many eggs in one basket. So, we made a public offer of a third of our shares – and that's the money we used to buy the oil. The gambles of course were punts but ones which frankly were no brainers – little downside risk and lots of possible upside. Our share of the Baldens' dividend is around £200 million a year. We have piles of cash in the bank from the share sale and we have never borrowed a penny. So, even now that Michael is cranking up the spending machine like crazy, there's still plenty to go round, at least for now."*

Andrew then asked a few questions about the two other revenue sources but it quickly became apparent that even the £60 million or so they had got back on an initial outlay of around half that, on the oil venture, was small beer overall. The rest of the morning was spent going through The Foundation's returns to the Charity Commission, the external auditors' written reports and the limited private bank and dealing accounts that The Foundation chose to have. Andrew could see very quickly that – although the visit had been eminently useful – there was little here for him.

Andrew met a couple of the other workers and succeeded in persuading Mo to go out for a long (and actually quite good) late lunch at a local Indian restaurant. Mo seemed relaxed and was clearly enjoying the departure from his normal daily routine. Over lunch, Andrew raised obliquely the two issues that he still felt unclear about. *"These Balden brothers must be great believers in what Michael stands for"* he said reflectively, taking a long draft of Kingfisher beer. Mo, who was drinking Diet Coke, smiled *"Yes, that's right. Of course, once Michael had the shareholding, he was pretty safe – the brothers had committed. Word around is that, in addition to the finance that Michael drummed up for them in the early days, some of the early Angel girls were, how shall I say, very solicitous to the brothers. But, to all intents and purposes that has long passed – if it ever happened at all. The Balden brothers live as recluses abroad now and have left all the hard work for years to a professional management that* so far have done a great job. We are at risk from a downturn in the retail food market; but people have to eat and we are with one of the best supermarket operators there is."

Andrew then took the conversation on to Mo himself. *"You've told me a bit about yourself, Mo. But how did you come to be doing this job? What brought you to the Angels?"* Mo leant back in his chair. *"It's no secret. I got involved with what are now the Muslim Angels about 3 years ago; and then came the whole issue of the Muslim and non-Muslim bits getting together. Don't get me wrong. I'm an Angel through and through. But you could regard my being here as part of the merger deal – so that Jibril and the people I report to under him could be sure that the cash side was OK. I'd had about 10 years' experience in the City. This job, with its complete change of pace, appealed; and I had a CV that normally would have merited a couple of hundred thousand basic from any self-respecting investment bank. So I took a pay cut and have seen a huge improvement in my quality of life – I've even settled down and married a non-Muslim Angel. And Michael got a quality resource for a fraction of the normal price – which is kind of par for his course."*

With that, and with a good deal to think over, Andrew climbed back into his car after lunch. He could hope to beat the worst of the London evening rush hour but not all of it. The day had not produced what he had expected.

14

Within 24 hours, Chloe had got in touch again. *"Michael says he hopes you got what you wanted at The Foundation. He's got another little job for you; I'd better come round and explain."* Which she did.

She refused his offer of coffee or something stronger. Andrew was getting used to her rather off-hand matter, though he was happy enough just to have here there; either she did just lift **his** mood when he saw her, or she did genuinely light up wherever she was. But it was good just to have her around.

Without much preamble, Chloe passed on the message for Andrew. *"Michael says he'd like you to help at one of the places we maintain for people who really need our help. They may have been uncontrollably into drink and drugs. We often take people, especially girls, who need to rebuild their self-confidence, often by way of a long detox with a bit of cosmetic surgery, often major weight loss and a dress make-over. I've been a patient in one of those courses, Andrew"* her voice faltered momentarily *"I'd touched a bottom in my life from which I thought there was no way up. And anything I have today is thanks to the three months or so I spent on that course. No"* she held up her hand, forestalling a remark or question from Andrew. *"Maybe another time I'll tell you but not now.*

These make-overs are expensive – when you add in all the cost of the places, the surgery, image make-overs and the rest. And nearly every penny gets paid for by the Angels. The results? A pretty tough and gruelling experience for those on the programme. But we're careful who we choose and about 80% of the men and mostly women who start a course finish it, though maybe not always as far forward on the road to recovery as we and they would like. Lots of the women Angels came to the ranks after experiencing this; once I had benefitted and got out, I committed my life to Michael the very next time I saw him because he had given me back a worthwhile life. And of course, though I don't suppose it'll get mentioned, quite a few of the men and women who will voluntarily be 'coming out' to back the Angels in the next few months will have had experiences very similar to mine."

"Fine" said Andrew *"But what am I supposed to be doing?"* *"Well"* Chloe replied *"Michael wants you to understand that sometimes a committed Angel has to do things they would rather not do – like Jenny with the footballer. In your case, Michael wants you to go down to our hide-away near Aldershot where the next survivors of the latest course come up for breath this weekend. What typically happens is that one or two are marked as the people who have made the most of their course and effectively 'won'. For the women, that usually involves a*

complete new free wardrobe, lots of alcohol if they want (which they won't have seen for months) and at least 1 desirable man. That's going to be you and they DO usually expect that. He wants you to be the main women's prize for a couple of nights at the end of this course. In that way, he wants you to understand that – if you were ever to be an Angel in the Inner Circle – you will sometimes have to do things you'd really rather not do. Like, in this case, having two very 'active' nights with a couple of women you've never met before. These girls can be a bit wild – I know I was when I got out – you have to 'ride the storm' if that's not too unfortunate a way of putting it."

Andrew couldn't think of anything to say. The fact that Chloe was here, talking so matter-of-factly about this subject, and her own past involvement was shock enough. Andrew turned the suggestion over in his mind; and the more he thought about it, the more he mentally cursed Michael's logic. Here was a proposal that couldn't be described as illegal even if it was unsavoury. And it was something that Michael knew Andrew could perfectly well do, if he had the stomach for it. But did he?

15

The following Friday, Chloe drove Andrew down to a village just outside Aldershot. As before, Andrew was struck by the little publicity given to there being any Angel-related activity here at all and by the serenity that seemed to surround him as he got out of the car.

The manager here – Mandy – was probably the oldest Angel he had met so far. She was a matronly figure who, within minutes, Andrew could see would probably be brilliant for the job in hand; watching over and coaxing forward people needing to rebuild their self-esteem and their lives. He felt like telling her his own life story quite unbidden!

Mandy explained that the latest course was ending with the awards ceremony that evening. Both the 'winners' of this course were women and Mandy quickly ran through what they had achieved. *"Both have been here for about 4 months. In that time, both have shed about 20% of their body weight. I won't bore you with the details; but some scientists came up with a fascinating discovery a few years ago; which is that obese people lose a lot of their taste buds, which in turn inclines them to eat more. We think we've found a way to restore those buds and therefore make weight loss both easier and more lasting.*

Anyway, both women have become really physically fit, had a complete make-over to their life-style, wardrobe and outlook on life. Sally has qualified to drive a truck which is what she has always wanted to do; Shirl has completed a quite tricky French language course and is well on the way to finishing her training as a nanny, which is what she has always wanted to do. You'll find both of them great; but, equally, both have been on a pretty tight rein for these last four months so they'll be, shall we say, in seriously celebratory mood. I think you should be with Sally tonight, Shirl tomorrow. We've set aside a little room where you can leave your stuff and, maybe, get a bit of extra sleep during the day tomorrow. We really appreciate what you're doing and I think you may enjoy it more than your look now suggests you think you will......."

As Chloe drove Andrew back to London on Sunday evening, two days later, Andrew had mixed feelings over what Mandy had said. If Sally handled her lorry as she had handled him on Friday evening, he pitied any trucker who got in her way in her new life. Shirl, in contrast, had been quite sweet, though demanding; and fortunately for him, Andrew had indeed managed to get a bit of down time and sleep during the day on Saturday. What he had established with both girls, though, was

101

just how miserable their lives had been before starting this course and what incredible personal efforts they had put in, during the course, to get as far as they had. As Shirl said *"I used to wake up in the morning – at 6.30 – and imagine all the unpleasant things I could do to my instructors when they put me through the hoops during the day. By 7pm each evening, I was so physically and mentally shattered that even those thoughts of revenge couldn't keep me going. Thank God, that's when they brought out the life-style and other changes, so that – when I finally fell asleep exhausted around 10 pm – my head would once again be filled with hope that I, me, **I** could get where I wanted. Nearly all the girls who began 3-4 months ago kept going. We all know we are going to need continuing contact with Angels as we go forward. But we have made friends for life – and not just among the girls but with our tormentors too."*

Chloe hadn't asked him anything about how the weekend had gone, when she reappeared on Sunday to drive him home. He had come to expect – and much liked – the secret smile that often lit up her face at times like that. Andrew always read it as saying 'I've been there, I know how you're thinking'. He also always fervently hoped that this was all part of a bonding process where, one day, she might say to him the things he longed to say to her.

16

This time, Andrew didn't have to do anything to get his reward for the second labour. He had told Chloe, on the way home, that he wanted to meet one of the key policy people who advised Michael. Around 10 a.m. Tuesday, this very individual – Matthew – was on the phone to Andrew, inviting him to come and visit the Policy Unit, which it turned out, was housed in one of the less fashionable parts of West London.

"I don't feel like trogging out to see you" Andrew said. *"Is there any chance you could come to me? I'll throw in a good long lunch if you do."* By now, Andrew had realised that the Angels, at least the non-Muslim ones, certainly had no aversion to alcohol or good food. Andrew reckoned a boozy lunch would be just the way to open this guy up and it could probably go on the Colonel's expense

account; and indeed Matthew jumped at the chance. Andrew gave Matthew the name of a good gastropub within about a mile of his flat; and they agreed to meet there at noon on Thursday.

Andrew gave little thought to how he would play this. His basic idea would be to ask a few open-ended questions and sit back, let Matthew take the conversation where he would. Matthew proved to be a small wiry individual, of around 30, with sparkling brown eyes and that inner peace that seemed to accompany most Angels he had met. Andrew had never really got close to the policy wonk at Michael's weekend; and, after preliminary pleasantries, Andrew thought the lunch would be enjoyable even if it didn't prove particularly enlightening.

Matthew – who made it clear from the outset that he preferred to be known as 'Matt' – also made clear at the outset that he had as much time as Andrew would need and that he liked both red wine and a good steak. Within 45 minutes, Andrew and he were well into a good bottle of Beaujolais and what promised to be excellent fillet steaks. Matt briefly sketched in his own history, which was basically that he had left university with a degree that brought him little in the way of worthwhile career opportunities, and had joined the Civil Service for around 5 years. By that point, it had become obvious to him – and to his bosses – that he was totally unsuited to working in a large bureaucracy or to toeing a policy line which he did not endorse 100%. Fortunately for Matt, by that point, he had met and started dating a girl who had been drawn into the Angel web. To help keep her, but also because the more he saw of Michael the more he liked what he heard, Matt had eventually become a full-time policy adviser for the Angels. The connections he had made in the Civil Service gave him a partial ready-made contact circle, to get him started on some of the policy issues he was now being asked to address.

Andrew listened with interest, not least because he could see the parallel between Matt's case and his own in respect of Chloe. *"So, what happens?"* asked Andrew, refilling Matt's wine glass. *"How does policy get formulated, agreed and disseminated? How much have you covered? I guess, over the next year you are going to have to come out with policies right across the board, if you want to convince the electorate that the Angels offer a safe pair of hands?"*

Matt paused, with a good-sized piece of steak on his fork. *"Well, it works roughly like this. Michael has given us a series of 'propositions' – we call then the Five Commandments – that all Angel policy has to be able to show it will meet. Basically simple things like the policy must be non-discriminatory; it must produce clear social welfare benefits overall even if not for every group affected. A connecting theme is of 'reasonableness'; what we think we can sell to voters as 'reasonable'. There are also some 'nice to have' features of policy like 'smaller Government rather than larger' and, wherever possible, we feed off work we already do – like the rehab courses. We want to show that, if we were able to get our hands on the massive resources that Government currently uses, we could get more bang per buck spent, or a better bang.*

Finally, there are a few no-go areas, perhaps the biggest being defence and health plus nothing ever on the Royal Family! No Angel would ever welcome violence but Michael concluded a long time ago that the average voter still wants the UK to pack a major military punch, even if no-one can think of circumstances in which we might use that punch without the Americans. So basically more bang per buck, literally for defence. Likewise the NHS. No-one in their right minds would argue that the NHS does not need drastic reform, and more money in some areas less in others; but again, in modern politics, it's just impossible to discuss changes like that sensibly. We are just going to have to get in power and make changes incrementally."

Matt renewed his enthusiastic attack on both the meat and the wine. *"So, we start with the Commandments; we draw up a series of ideas, these go back and forth – first with Michael and then with test panels of Angels and voters. Out of that eventually comes a set of policy proposals, with the line always being that, in some areas quite reasonably, we can't possibly put up details until we get our hands on the levers of power."*

"Could you take me through one or two areas to show how that is working?" asked Andrew. *"I presume in most cases, you haven't gone public on much yet, as that will need to await the run-up to the Election. But, as I'm sure you've been told, you should treat me as an insider. And I promise that what you tell me won't go further than this restaurant."* (Unless you count what I'm going to tell the Colonel, added Andrew mentally.)

"Hmm" said Matt. *"Well let's start with tax policy. To listen to public debate, you'd think that everyone wants to spend more money on almost everything you could think of but not pay more tax themselves. The work we've done suggests a quite different picture. The Tories aren't trusted because many voters think any extra money the Tories spend will go to their sharp-*

suited business 'friends'. Labour are thought to be untrustworthy, that they will waste any money they spend. Likewise, on tax. What concerns most people is that the present system is manifestly unfair. Rich foreigners and multinational companies for example play the tax avoidance/evasion game brilliantly and successive UK Governments have effectively turned a blind eye. Out of that mix, it's not actually hard to come up with a set of proposals that suggest lower overall rates of marginal tax but stops the really rich and well-advised wriggling out, paying next to nothing. A bit like your footballer but on a huge scale." Not for the first time, Andrew realised that literally everything he did with an Angel somehow seemed to get on the news circuit they had among themselves. If he ever got access to this 'magic circle', was he going to have fun finding out what Chloe and the others were up to – and what they had thought of him!

Matt went on. *"Of course, in the event, there will be a whole lot of shouting if such policies are ever introduced. Rich Russians and Arabs threatening to leave London; places like the Cayman Islands screaming about the impact on cutting out tax havens; big multinationals saying they'll stop selling coffee in London or hold back on bringing in new high-tech gadgets to their shops. But we think – and more importantly we think we can show voters – that this is nearly all hot air. Across the globe, for example, multinationals currently pay less than 10% of their profits in tax to any Government; and even that money often goes to Governments, like the Irish, who don't provide the 'home front' where these profits are actually earned.*

Now, take something quite different – reforming Parliament. Despite changes in recent years, most people still think there are far too many snouts in the trough, drawing pay and expenses.

Everyone who thinks about it knows really that Westminster needs to be shut and refurbished properly over about five years to make it habitable again, although you'd never get the current rabble of MPs to agree that. Our policies – which will include big cuts in the number of MPs and in the House of Lords, 5 years for Parliament in Birmingham while Westminster is redone – will go down a storm with most voters. And –perhaps most important – it will leave the main parties completely at sea, as they have spent years defending what is essentially indefensible.

Another incredibly popular policy will be one of the first policy changes we will make in this area, which is that no Angel MP will draw a salary or ask for expenses (instead these will be paid for by the Angel Foundation, not out of the public purse). All our policy testing suggest that these ideas will get a great reception, while at the same time burnishing the reputation we want for being practical and thrifty. Some of them will play better outside London than in it; but to be honest we're not expecting miracles from London constituencies, so that probably doesn't matter."

By this time, they had polished off the steaks and the first bottle of wine. Andrew was enjoying sitting back and letting all this flow over him, especially as he agreed with most of the specifics that Matt came up with. They moved on to dessert, high-calorie disasters but Andrew, for one, had been going easy on the calories for a bit so he didn't care. He ordered a second bottle of wine. And by the time they had drunk that, and had coffee, Andrew was ready to pour himself into the street and say farewell for now to Matt, who seemed to have enjoyed the whole thing immensely. This had been a painless, indeed pleasant, way to spend half a day.

17

When he had sobered up later that evening, Andrew reckoned that, even if he hadn't got much new to offer the Colonel, the lunch had still been worthwhile. In particular, it had established that Michael was serious about going into the next Election with a range of policies prepared; and that his bravado was backed up by something thought out. What in fact the Electorate would make of the detail of some of these policies, only time would tell. But, as Mark had made clear, the Angel hope was that the main parties would not try to throw the spotlight on the plausibility or economics of an Angel platform until near the Election, preferring instead in the early months to go on scoring points off each other. They were relying too that on the specifics of what the Angels had done thus far (the rehab schemes, the young family facilities and so on), they would be able to show that they had delivered value using their own money and improving lives.

The next development was unexpected. Andrew got a call directly from one of Michael's inner circle, to say that – if he were free – a car would pick him up the next morning, as 'Michael needs to see you'. Andrew wasn't going to miss a chance like that and readily agreed without pressing further, other than to establish that an overnight stay wasn't needed.

As arranged, a car – with a taciturn but not unfriendly driver – turned up for him at 10.30 the next morning; and he found himself retracing the steps Chloe had taken a couple of weeks earlier. Andrew was obviously going to meet Michael again where he had before.

By the time he arrived, it was 12.30 and he was promptly met by a Sister and taken straight into lunch. This was rather like the meals Andrew had attended before, good food, self-service, open and business-like. There were about 20 other people there and, in the distance, Andrew could see that one of them was the policy wonk 'Matt'. Perhaps this was one of their days for talking over and testing out some of the policies being created.

Michael himself wasn't there. But immediately after lunch, Andrew was ushered into one of the side rooms off the dining area, where he found Michael seated, alone. The man looked a little tired, or perhaps preoccupied was a better word. But Michael turned in his chair, and bade Andrew sit down. *"Well done with the first 2 labours. I hope you got what you wanted in return, as your reward"* said Michael. *"We need to talk about the third and final labour."*

Andrew made clear that was fine by him. Michael sat quietly for a couple of minutes and then began. *"I was going to ask you to take on what is probably a rather thankless and quite lengthy task. We've been working for some time on one of the more intractable problems of recycling. You know we're pretty hot on environmental issues; and one of the best ways we can show voters, especially the Millennials, that we are different from the rest, is to give evidence of **how** we would be different. We've done most of the easy part. We persuaded Baldens ages ago, for example, to revamp their packaging, cut waste and make it easy to recycle. We can readily show that this is one way for everyone to go.*

But we've also had scientists and engineers working for some time now on one of the really tricky problems, which is that plastic waste, when it comes in for recycling, is a hotchpotch of different kinds of plastic. The heavier plastics can typically be ground, washed and melted down, to turn into pellets that eventually can be used to produce bottles and similar things. The main problem has been that the different types of plastic aren't compatible. I'll spare you a physics lesson. But, for example, polyvinyl chloride – PVC to you which you'll find in cling film, say – degrades polyethylene terephthalate, PET, which you'll find in plastic bottles; and vice versa.

Now, we've made a breakthrough that will allow much more plastic to be sorted and reused, though I have to admit even we can't do it yet on a basis that makes much commercial sense. And we're building a new recycling plant on the coast to demonstrate it. Trouble is none of that is very news-worthy or photogenic. Hence why I thought of you.

Someone's first idea was that we should kit out a boat to

111

harvest plastic from the area that is now known as 'the sea of plastic' because there is so much rubbish there. Unfortunately, no-one thought through the implications. The sea of plastic is a huge area between California and Hawaii. How would we get the boat out there in ecologically acceptable fashion, collect the stuff and then get it back to our new 'factory'? I can see it would have made good TV; and we got an independent company interested, who are sure in turn that they can on-sell it to the BBC. But they're primarily interested in our new processes, so we've come up with a much better idea – scavenge a lot of plastic that's already here in the UK, get that to the factory and do the TV programme about that.

Now, to do that, we will need an articulate, photogenic individual on our side, to lead it – organise the scavenging parties, explain what is being done and so on. And I thought of you. But, at the last moment, another suitable candidate has appeared and, anyway, I wanted you to see something rather different about our operations in your third labour.

So, it'll be your choice." and here Michael drew breath and paused. *"Leading this TV programme OR we could blood you in something quite different that would admit a side of us you haven't yet seen. One for which an Angel close to our hearts, sadly, may need to be prepared.*

Before I explain exactly what 'something' that is, I need to make clear that we stand for non-violence and due process. But, even for an organisation like us, there arises very occasionally a situation where non-violence and due process won't get you where you need to be. So, more than with the second labour, if you really want to be a key player in our organisation, I need you to understand that it may occasionally be necessary for us to take the law into our own hands.

This case is the result of an aggravated rape of one of our girls, a few months ago. The boy – he's about 20 – who did it is a gang leader and small-time drug dealer. The rape was probably not premeditated but the boy was clever – and prepared enough – to use a condom; so no bodily fluids that the police could pick up on. And he quickly set himself up an alibi with some of his crooked friends. The girl did report it, when she had recovered. But, though we have friends in the local police, all we've got back from them is that there isn't enough evidence to bring him to trial. I think we owe it to the girl to teach this boy such a lesson that, just maybe, he will never do any such thing again.

What I'm asking of you is that you join a small team – two other professionals – who are planning a suitable lesson for the boy. I promise you that he won't be permanently disabled or hurt; but, nevertheless, violence – or at least the threat of it – will be necessary. We aim to do it in a way that ideally will never even get to the police or, if it does, will not lead them back to us. Small-time drug dealers tend to have lots of enemies – the police know that well enough. And, anyway, I understand the plan is to exact a penalty that, if he's sensible, the boy will never even acknowledge, let alone seek remedy with the authorities.

That's the choice. I've always tried to be straight with you. Even if you choose the voyage to sea, you will now be aware that even the Angels have a small, rarely exposed, darker side. I think it's no bad thing that you understand it. I discussed this second option with Chloe. She thought you were mature enough to have worked out for yourself that we can't always be whiter than white; and she also thought that, provided you met with the girl and heard her story first-hand, you might feel sufficiently angry to join us. Your call. I'll leave you for an hour to think about it; and I know Chloe is going to drop in on you in the next few minutes."

With that, Michael left and Andrew was, in turn, left with very mixed emotions. He was at heart a military man, or at least his training had been. He had done considerably worse things he reflected during his spell of active duty; like shooting a man who he was sure was a terrorist but who hadn't been through any due legal process to establish that he was. This, however, would be much more cold-blooded. And, Andrew's mind was always intensely practical, how likely was it that the affair could end badly? With the Colonel needing to come in and literally bail him out of trouble?

Andrew felt rather than heard the door behind him open. And then, there was Chloe. *"I hope you don't think too badly of me"* she said. *"I have been in the same place – about four years ago- to where you are now. I concluded then that the Angels do such good – and can do so much more – that, if I had to cross a line occasionally for them then I would. In practice, it has only been necessary a couple of times; and in both cases, like what I know of this rape, I was so angry with the target that I've never had a sleepless night. No pressure, Andrew; and I'll go now. But I do want you to stay and thrive in the Angels. I do want you, like me, to be part of the inner circle. Let's just say I'd miss you a lot if you go."* She left as quietly as she had come.

Andrew weighed up his options. If he really couldn't stomach the second option then he should effectively say so by walking out and refusing either part of the challenge. He knew that, if the Colonel were here, he would be urging him to go on. He knew also that, whatever Chloe had meant in saying she would 'miss him', his heart had leapt when she had said those words. One of the very few nice personal things he now realised that she had ever said to him.

All in all, there was no real choice to be made. He would meet the girl and, provided he believed her story and her being able to ID the man who had done it, he would be 'in'. That was the short answer he gave Michael when the latter returned a while later.

18

Subsequent events moved rapidly. That evening, Andrew was rung at home. A male voice introduced himself as John and gave Andrew some quick explicit instructions. Within 30 seconds, Andrew had realised John must be one of his two new companions in crime. *"Come to the following address"* (This was somewhere on the outskirts of Manchester by the sound of it.) *"Bring a couple of changes of dark clothes – ones that are easy to take on and off and which you won't mind losing. You'll only need to be here 2-3 days. We've been working on this for weeks. Now you happen along and get the benefit of our work. By the way, I presume you can drive any small van we may be needing? Having you as our driver will muck us up less, if – as I'm assured – you are properly trained. And safer for us than involving you more fully."*

Andrew acknowledged that he should be able to drive anything they needed. And he also felt constrained to point out that it wasn't him, Andrew, who had inserted himself at the last minute. *"I'll be with you by mid-afternoon tomorrow. I presume you'd like me to come by public transport and leave no footprint of the journey? And, by the way as I hope you've been told, I want to meet with the girl"* he searched for the right words *"that we're helping. Fix that for tomorrow if you can."*

Andrew rang off. The caller had been brusque to the point of rudeness. But Andrew could see that, from the latter's point of view, having another operative inserted into the operation at the last minute must be frustrating.

Thanking Google, not for the first time, Andrew then checked up on the journey he would need and on a couple of Manchester-related sites. He logged out, using the tool which the Colonel had given him several years ago, to expunge (as far as possible) his footprint round the web. He then went out and got himself £1,000 in cash out of the local ATM – lucky he lived near the City where such cash demands were not uncommon; he had already established that a First Class Anytime Return from Euston to Manchester Piccadilly was nearly £500. He certainly wasn't going Standard Class and he needed to pay cash. A couple of drinks down at his local, a quick selection of suitable clothes including a balaclava and a suitcase. And he was ready.

From past sorties, he knew that there were no labels on any of the clothing that could, if the worst came to the worst, tie back to him. And he went carefully through the pockets to make sure there was nothing there either.

His fingerprints he would be bound to leave around, likewise the odd hair or piece of sloughed skin. But, again from past operations, he knew that no official data base held any record to which this data could be tied back to him. He was good to go. Last, he added in what he always called his 'trouble pack' – which should really have been the 'get out of trouble' pack. Gloves, torch, matches – a handful of things that he had previously found invaluable. Nothing that would cause comment if looked at by an outsider. Certainly no weapons, unless you counted the rather elaborate Swiss Army knife which was something he wasn't going to leave out and which, to most people, would seem innocent enough.

He talked briefly with Chloe, saying only that he would be away on Angel business for a few days. And then he slept, soundly and dreamlessly. The journey up to Manchester was uneventful – except for the fact that the train was on time (he didn't know the line, so really had no idea whether that was usual or not). He had the subsequent bus route in his head. And, though the bus passed the address he had been given, he descended about half a mile before that and walked through the streets, to get at least a feel of the neighbourhood – rather down at heel suburban city.

The address itself was an end of terrace two storey building, probably built in the 1930s, quite unremarkable at least from the outside. It was John, it turned out, who opened the door to him and wordlessly ushered him into the main living room. There he met the other member of the team, Jake. Both John and Jake looked exactly like the kind of men you would go out of your way to avoid on a dark evening. Andrew decided they were probably both special ops trained in the Army and that he would go down best with them, if he cut a serious and workman-like face for them. The kind his own Army training had prepared him for. They probably needed reassurance that he wasn't some rookie who was going to compromise whatever they had planned.

Very limited pleasantries were exchanged. John offered coffee, which Andrew accepted and they sat silent, rather incongruously Andrew thought given the circumstances.

John eventually spoke (and, indeed subsequently, Andrew could hardly recall a word that Jake spoke then, or later). *"I've fixed for you to meet the girl, Julie, early evening in the local pizza restaurant. It needs to be today because we have the action planned for Sunday evening; and the girl will be 200 miles from here by Sunday morning so that, if any attempt were later made by the police to link her to the attack, she would have a clear alibi. The action will take place, if things go according to plan, in the back room of the pizza place; they open as a restaurant on Saturday but only do takeaway Sunday. If you meet her, as I've suggested around 7, you'll get a chance to size up the place. The two boys who run the place are 'friends'. They won't know who you are and it should stay that way; but they won't be unfriendly if they see you with the girl, put it like that.*

As for Sunday, all you need to know I think is that you will drive us in a small van that we have garaged near here, to the back of the restaurant around 7 tomorrow evening. There's a back entrance. Jake and I will go in. You will wait in the car ready to drive away when we get out. The little bastard we're after is due to drop in around then – the pizza boys have been his drug collection point for the last few months. He's a suspicious little runt, so the chances are he'll bring either no-one or just his one reasonably trusted helper, which couldn't be better from our point of view. We have an Angel inside their gang. He will know when the kid leaves their hole and can warn us if anything goes wrong.

There's a small stretcher already in the restaurant. We will knock the kid out (and his helper if he has one). Chemically if possible, Jake's a dab hand with the needle, physically if not. We carry him out to the back of the van, tell you where to drive and that's the first part done.

We then drive to another safe house about 5 miles away which has a garage. To anyone who notices us there – and people round here tend to keep their noses out of neighbours' business – we'll look like three guys going round for drinks and maybe a porn movie, before another long boring week at work. In the house is a kitchen where another mate of ours, who knows how to handle a different set of needles, tattooing, will be waiting.

Our little friend will be lucky. Jake will make sure he sleeps through what would otherwise be quite a painful little operation, while our friend tattoos a suitable message down the back of each leg and across his chest. We'll be filming the outcome – we shall want our friend to realise when he wakes up that he has a real choice. He can keep quiet and the film stays off his social media. Or he can go to the fuzz and report the attack. He hates the police, they hate him. So our guess is that he'll keep quiet; but we'll see. Anyway when the tattooist has done his stuff, he'll get back to his base. All he needs with him is a set of needles, bandages, antiseptic and the needle machine. The latter is hand-held, a doddle. We will load the boy up in the van; you drive out, drop him in a suitable country lane a few miles away and leave him to sleep it off.

When he wakes up, he can decide for himself whether he walks home and keeps quiet, or not. We'll be back in London, the van gets a make-over to look like it did Friday, the genuine number plates put back on. Bob's your uncle. Oh, and by the way, don't worry about the local CCTV. We have friends again who will put that out for the relevant period, not that there's much CCTV anyway in poor areas like the pizza joint – not enough valuable to protect. And Vehicle Registration cameras down the motorway and so on, no problem. What will they be looking for? By early Monday morning when we aim to do the trip, there'll be 300 white vans an hour bombing up and down the M6 and we're legit.

Of course things can go wrong. But I have to say that my experience of the Angels has been pretty good so far. If the CCTV is supposed to be out it will be; and I rather suspect the local police will have a few other call-outs on Sunday evening to deal with, even if something goes wrong and a passer-by or neighbour sees something and does report it in. Life gets a little more complicated if he brings a helper; but only a little."

"All sounds straightforward" commented Andrew. "Certainly beats yomping through some bloody desert" – Jake made his only contribution to the conversation. Andrew continued "I'll see the girl and then come back here – I presume we're sleeping here. What if the kid does call it in on Monday? He'll be able to lead the police straight to the pizza takeaway which gives them a flying start."

"Yes" replied John. "But our Angel friends don't do things by halves. The two pizza lads will also be taking off Sunday night as soon as we've left and they're disappearing down south.

They're being well paid. The restaurant has got all sorts of bills outstanding; and doing a runner, if you have a place like that on a lease where the rent is behind, isn't exactly uncommon. I tried to work out at one point how much the Angels have spent on getting come-uppance for this kid – it must be well over 50 grand plus what we're getting. Pretty impressive!"

"One last question" said Andrew. *"What actually is the message that the kid's going to get?* "Very boring" John replied with a slight smile. *"On the back of one leg 'small time' on the other 'crook'; across his chest 'dealer'. It has to be there; we think he's already got traditional tattoos on his arms. I wanted the message just to say 'rapist' but the powers that be thought that too much of a giveaway as to where the attack might have come from, if the kid does call it in. This way, it can look to an outsider like the whole thing was just a typical 'small gang/dealer spat'. But, in one of the brief periods when the boy's awake, we will make it clear why it's being done. And we will be saying that, if in future we hear a word about him abusing **any** girl, we'll be back for his balls.*

Look, he's being really lucky. We'll make sure the tattoo can't easily be got rid of, apparently that's best done by using coloured inks rather than just black. But he'll be getting washed, antiseptic, bandages – all the gear just like he would if he were paying for this in a parlour. And, as I say, he'll be asleep during the bit that might hurt. Personally, I shan't mind him if I have to give him an additional kick or two, if he's not 100% co-operative. I think the Angels are pussy-footing on this, to be honest."

Andrew left, as he had said he would, around 6.30. He had been told where he would find the restaurant and how he could recognise the girl and exchange a coded greeting. It was only about 10 minutes' walk; and he spent the next 20 minutes or so reconnoitring the main street and the alley that obviously led to the back of the restaurant. The alley would give him a degree of cover from being seen from the road; and anyway, Andrew reasoned, the whole area would be used to seeing cars waiting or parked near the restaurant. Takeaway round here probably meant most orders being collected from the restaurant; rather than delivered by the restaurant itself.

The two young men running the shop sounded like South Africans. There were only a handful of tables but Andrew chose one in the corner furthest away from the pick-up counter, and ordered a soft drink (no alcohol licence he noted). There was hardly anyone else around but, anyway, when Julie arrived, Andrew didn't need a second look to decide that she was the girl he was waiting for. He rose quickly, went over to her and introduced himself *"I'm the guy that Chloe will have told you about – probably best we don't mention my name. Come and sit down and, if you're hungry, let's eat."*

One thing John hadn't mentioned was that the pizza was actually pretty good, as Andrew was able to attest to after they had shared a Four Seasons and a 'Spicy Special', together with two mixed salads and further soft drink. Initially they chatted inconsequentially – Andrew hadn't given much thought to how he would gain her confidence. But he had determined that she shouldn't know anything about him – just in case things went wrong tomorrow.

Actually, the link with Chloe provided the key he needed. When Julie found out that he knew Chloe quite well, it was a natural segue to Julie explaining how much she had come to depend on Chloe, after what she persisted for the next 45 minutes in always referring to as 'the evening it happened'. What Andrew wanted to know was that she was a credible witness, so that when she described the young dealer and what had happened, Andrew should have no doubt that it really had happened and that the boy really had been responsible.

That Julie had no difficulty in demonstrating to Andrew. The boy had mitigated his actions by using a condom and by keeping the rest of his gang out of the room while the assault took place. Within 10 minutes, Andrew was convinced that Michael had given him a true bill of what had happened. It took rather longer for Andrew to feel reassured that, though Julie had clearly suffered panic attacks and all kinds of problems afterwards, she was now at least partly healed; and, as Andrew realised he had come subconsciously to expect, that the Angels had stood by her all the way through the recovery process. *"That's where Chloe was so great – always there when I needed, always supportive but never pushy or demanding"* commented Julie as they finished the pizzas. *"And"* she smiled wanly as she waved her hands at the now empty plates in front of them *"at least you can see I've got my appetite back."*

At no point did Julie ask anything about why Andrew was there or what was being planned. Indeed, Andrew never found out if she knew what was in train or indeed whether she had ever asked the Angels to do anything. Like several Angels he'd met in his weeks with them, she radiated almost unquestioning trust in what the Angels thought and did. Naïve? Sensible in the circumstances? Who could say. But, at least Andrew concluded that, even if the attack happened, and was reported and was somehow linked back to the attack on Julie, there was no active lead beyond that to John, Jake or him.

Julie declined an offer to transfer from the restaurant to a local pub. She thanked him for the evening and quietly left. Andrew found himself back at the suburban semi by 9, though not before he had stocked up on some wine and whisky to get them through the evening. Even Jake, he thought, would welcome that way of passing the time.

The time did pass and – indeed more slowly – the daylight hours of Sunday. John allowed him to get Sunday papers the next morning; and Jake cooked a large fry-up early afternoon, in best Army tradition, so that the operation would not take place on empty stomachs. Early evening, with John in charge throughout, they shut the house down and John gave Andrew about 30 minutes to get acquainted with the van they would be using that evening. *"Don't want you stalling, or going into reverse, or something equally crass"* John noted.

The van had two front seats and a narrow back seat where one person (Jake) could stretch out in reasonable comfort. John guided Andrew to the restaurant and checked that he knew where to wait when the time came. Thanks to Andrew's reconnaissance the night before, this took very little time. John then handed Andrew a small mobile phone *"Pay as you go – programmed with just 2 numbers you can ring, Jake and me. Don't use it unless something really vital goes wrong. Now, drop us and bugger off.*

The kid isn't due for at least an hour but I don't want him seeing this van stuck behind the restaurant when he comes, nor indeed you waiting there for very long. Unless I call you, just turn up behind the restaurant and park at 8, keep the engine ticking over and wait. The restaurant will have a notice on the door saying it's closed. Very appropriate given that they're going to do a flit and we don't want anyone dropping in unnecessarily while we're convincing the young man that he's going to come with us.

And that's all you have to do. We'll come out the back with the stretcher, shove it in the back of the van –it's unlocked, I've checked – and then Jake and I'll join you. I can then give you the next address to drive to, I know the route well. When we get there, you just drive into their garage which will be open. I'll get out and close the garage door; we can get the stretcher into the house without going outside. You come with us – I've arranged for you to kip down for a few hours – I don't want you driving us to London without having had a bit of sleep. About 3 hours later, we will have finished. But we'll wait until about 6 a.m., get you up with a bit of nosh. We'll get the kid back to the van; and then we can drop him somewhere nice and shady in the country to sleep it off. While you drive us back to London."

Amazingly, events followed the script very closely. The kid actually turned up a bit before time; but John and Jake were fully ready. The kid didn't bring anyone which – as John observed later – meant there was very little chance of anyone calling him into the police that night, as missing. Andrew did the driving he had been briefed for. He never even saw the boy's face – just the stretcher on which he was carried – nor indeed whoever was in the house they drove onto and who presumably carried out the tattooing. About 9 hours later Andrew

126

was easing the van onto the M6, with the kid safely left to sleep in a country lane that John had obviously picked out well before. Andrew wasn't sure whether the good result was a consequence of John's meticulous planning or just sheer bloody luck. But as Napoleon was supposed to have said 'Give me generals who are lucky'; so, Andrew thought, Michael and the Angels probably felt the same about their own operatives. Of which Andrew was now very much one.

19

John and Jake dropped Andrew off as soon as they reached the outskirts of the London Underground. Andrew had no desire to spend more time with them, nor that they should know where he lived. Nevertheless, he accepted that the operation had gone incredibly smoothly and that this must have been largely due to John's organisation and to the calm and professional way John and Jake had gone about it. So, as he climbed out of the van outside Uxbridge Tube Station, relinquishing the driving seat to John, he thought he should acknowledge what they had done and part on good terms.

So, he solemnly shook hands with each before he climbed out, thanked them for making his own part so easy and wished them luck for the future. Before John could remind him, Andrew dug the mobile phone out of his pocket, wiped it carefully for fingerprints and handed it over to John, holding it in his handkerchief as he did so. To his slight surprise, John actually smiled at him. *"Take care yourself"* said John. *"If, our lad does decide to go to the police, someone – not us – will ring and warn you. In the meantime, I suggest you get home, have a few beers and make sure that some Angel bird will give you an alibi – should you need one – for at least part of the weekend."* Andrew had already marked that as something to be arranged. And John and Jake departed.

A day or so later, Andrew had recovered his optimism (there *would* be little that could tie him to Manchester that weekend, if things did get hot). Chloe was more than happy to sketch in an alibi for him. And, thinking about it, Andrew also felt remarkably good about what he had just done. Helped no doubt by the fact that he hadn't even talked to the youth, let alone contributed directly to his 'punishment', Andrew felt that the boy had got no more than what was coming to him, indeed that he had got off lightly. The beers John had suggested he enjoy on getting home had actually been a bottle of Penfold 389, his favourite red wine. The cost for once could go hang. As he sat comfortably at home listening to his Sonos, he raised the first glass to Julie. *"We have paid him one back."*

Andrew also had a little time to think about the 'reward' for the third labour and had concluded that he might see if he could take a rain check on it. There was nothing he immediately wanted to follow up on. He thought tracking down some of Michael's immediate staff might be worth doing sometime; but he couldn't see that it was particularly appropriate right now. And something else might well come up that he wanted to do.

Thoughts like that drained from his mind when the phone went on Wednesday and a female voice at the other end asked if that was Andrew Davies. Andrew immediately thought this might be the one thing he had dreaded, a call to say that the police had become involved and that he should be on his guard.

Instead, having established that he was indeed the right person, the girl merely said that a car would be coming to pick him up – later that day if he was free; and that he should plan on being away just one night. Andrew said indeed he had nothing planned – which was only too true as he had wanted to talk further with Chloe properly before making his plans for the week ahead.

By 4 p.m. Andrew therefore found himself in a car which, it very quickly became clear, was again going to take him where he had been twice before. The traffic wasn't too heavy – they had just beaten the worst of the rush hour – but it was still after 6 when they arrived. As soon as he had walked in through the main door, a Sister appeared – one he had met before. *"Welcome back, Andrew. We've got the same room for you. Dinner will be at 7.30 and then the ceremony will be after that."* Andrew immediately asked *"What ceremony?"* The girl just smiled *"Sorry, ignore that. I shouldn't have said anything."*

Although it was the middle of the week, there appeared to be quite a few Angels around. And, when he

130

went down to dinner – the bell had sounded punctually at 7.30 as he knew now it would – he was happy to see that Chloe was there too. Even better, she came up to him and kissed him with a degree of enthusiasm she had never shown before. That wasn't just 'hello' to a friend, or at least so he hoped. She even sat next to him; and Andrew noticed that Chloe had a small amount of make-up on, something that he had rarely seen before.

Michael joined them for the meal; and the numbers were just small enough to allow them to sit round a circular table and talk together, though mostly that meant listening to Michael. As he listened, Andrew wondered to what extent Michael was talking to him; but, as things progressed, he decided that Michael was actually trying to raise spirits and lift the heads of all those present.

"We're growing faster now than at any time in the past" Michael said. *"I know that this puts strains on a lot of you. Having to help induct new recruits, constantly helping people who are still struggling to understand what we expect of them. As well, of course, as your 'day jobs', most of which require 100% focus on the period up to the Election. But let's look at it another way.*

The psychologists say that few of us are capable of making meaningful connections with more than about 150 people. More than that, you can't really get to know them or keep up with their own personal paths. You can't get a real feel for whether you can trust them or not, which is vital for us. We must be able to trust each other; and, when you meet a new Angel, you are really dependent on those who have met them and think they are worthy to join us.

Now, if you think about your own situations, you will probably find that you're at or near the 150 limit. But you'll also *probably find that this number breaks down into three groups: other Angels, family members plus old friends from before your Angel days and the group of people you are struggling to support and bring on. Now, it's a matter of simple arithmetic. Say that last group account for half of all those you have a relationship with. That's 75 for each of you. There are now over 150 Angels of the inner circle. If each has 75 outer contacts, that comes to 11,000 with some overlaps. If eventually, half of those 11,000 become Angels of the outer circle themselves – or at least are well disposed towards us, then you are looking at a total approaching 400,000 by the time you've added in all **their** non-family contacts. We can do a huge amount with even half that number working with us, canvassing and supporting our initiatives. Certainly that's a whole lot more than the main political parties could lay claim to. In short, it seems like hard work now, it **is** hard work. But we're making amazing progress.*

That leads me on to why many of us are really here tonight. With the Election coming so quickly, we have to move faster in selecting new people to join us than would be ideal. Just occasionally, though, new recruits appear who can be tried and tested in weeks rather than months and who will show very quickly whether or not they are worth our trust. We have one such here tonight and I'm going to ask an Angel of the Inner Circle to introduce that person to us."

Andrew felt rather than saw Chloe stand next to him. *"As many of you know, I have been an Angel of the Inner Circle for some years now. I met a man only about two months ago who I could see immediately might have huge talents to bring to our cause. He was dissatisfied with the world he found around him. He had physical and mental skills we need in abundance. I brought him here to meet Michael and to see if that would cause the spark that I could see within him to burst into life. It did.*

Michael has since then asked him to complete three tasks for us, showing him in the process that the life of an Angel may not be emotionally or morally smooth and simple. He has passed those tests with flying colours. Michael has confirmed that he is happy for this man to become not only an Angel but immediately an Angel of the Inner Circle. His name is Andrew Davies." And here Chloe turned to look at him. *"And I now ask him, in front of you all, whether he is ready and willing to take on the mantle he is being offered."* She sat down. It was obvious that now was the time for Andrew himself to speak.

He cleared his throat. *"I can honestly say that I have never been so caught on the hop as I am now. I had no idea that such an honour could be bestowed – especially not on one like me so new to your ranks. If I had known and had thought about the possibility, then I don't know exactly what I would have said."* He was silent for a moment. *"But now it has come like this, out of the blue, I can tell you that my heart is singing and every sinew in me wants to say 'yes, yes please.' I have seen some of you at work and I admire the things that the Angels have already done. I have listened to Michael and I have heard there a philosophy of hope and renewal. One which – though of course it will take time – could mean new and better lives for millions of those in this country, maybe eventually world-wide. So, that is my answer 'yes, yes please."*

Several Sisters had obviously been waiting at the side of the room. They now appeared with trays of drinks – either soft for a few or what turned out to be good champagne for Andrew himself and most of the others. Michael had sat watching Chloe and Andrew. He now

133

rose to his feet. *"We don't believe in elaborate ceremonies for things like this. I don't present a badge of office or drag out a pair of fake white wings for you to put on. All that will happen is that the bush telegraph – which is what I call the amazingly effective social media services we run for the Inner Circle, the Seraphim, and for Angels more generally – will do its job. It will have photos and CV up for you before you can get to your room. Now, I suggest we break this up. Andrew, I suggest you and Chloe retire for a chat – I have little doubt there are things you want to say to her, Andrew, starting perhaps with 'why did you spring that on me?' Take a full bottle of champagne with you, I happen to know this is Chloe's favourite and we'll see you for breakfast tomorrow."* With that, he smiled again and left the room.

20

Many of those present gathered round Andrew to offer their own congratulations. A few – like Gabrielle and Mo – he knew; the others were at best names to him. Eventually, he managed to edge to the door, clutching a bottle of champagne that a Sister had thrust firmly into his hand and, from there upstairs to what he had come to think of as his room, Number 3.

He sank down on the bed once inside, quite overcome by what had happened. A slew of thoughts ran through his mind – the fairly irrelevant (like how pleased the Colonel would be) to the important – what would this mean for him and Chloe? He soon got a possible answer to the second thought, as Chloe slipped into the room and stood smiling down at him. *"You obviously didn't see that coming but then why should you? I don't suppose there have been more than a handful of people who have moved from being an outsider to a Seraph in one go; and certainly not as quickly as you have managed it. So now you hold the record. The question now is whether you want another first to your name."*

She paused. Andrew stayed quiet – he had no idea what was coming though his heart was telling him that this could be his moment with her. She continued *"I've told you before that, now, I could never go with a non-Angel. I could never be a Watcher. But, also I don't want any more transient relationships with other Angels – I've had my fill of those. So my question to you now is whether you want to hook up with me? I can't expect you to commit wholly – anymore than I can at the moment. It will be enough if you want to become my partner, tell the Angel world that we are partners, and stay loyal to me until one of us changes our mind and breaks the relation. No more one-night stands for you. You would be the man I think I have already come to love and whom I could respect. You'd share my bed, we'd share our lives."*

Andrew's head spun – this was more than he could ever have hoped. He tried to speak but his throat was dry. Eventually, he managed to croak – to repeat what he had said to Michael a few minutes ago *"oh yes, yes please."* She stood up, she threw her arms around him; and, over the next hour, the pact was made and consummated, the champagne drunk.

21

When Andrew came to the next morning, his head initially declined to function. Chloe was gone, she had no doubt slipped out, but he did remember – in a cascade of memory – the events of last night, the wonder of being with Chloe and the happiness he had felt then and felt now. After a few minutes, he threw the duvet off, showered and briskly shaved before going down to breakfast. The meal, his watch told him, had probably been on the go for at least half an hour already.

There was no sign of Chloe and, as Andrew wanted no more than coffee and toast, he was through in about 10 minutes. Everyone around him smiled when they saw him but left him alone, for which he was grateful. He rose and went back to his room. Chloe would no doubt reappear when it suited her.

He must have dozed off for it was about an hour later when there was a quiet knock on the door. It was enough to waken him and he said, without thinking, *"Come in."* It was Freddy – whom he hadn't seen since the early days at the Oxford Circus shop – something which, although only just a few months ago, seemed to him like ancient history.

"Congratulations" said Freddy. *"You've got further in two months than I have in 5 years. But, if you're me, you get used to that. Anyway, it has its compensations, including my being able to come round this morning with the gear you're now going to need – and to answer any questions you may have.*

Gear first. From what I see in Chloe's blog, the first thing you need is this" – he held out 2 fairly thick armbands made up of green and yellow bands twisted together. *"One for you, one in case Chloe doesn't have one already. This is the band you need to display so that other Angels know that you're hooked up with another Angel. The others you've been wearing can get put away for now. Some couples go in for bands with each other's initials woven in. But most people think that's rather OTT; and anyway, nearly all the people who need to know about you will already know that you've hooked up with Chloe.*

Now, the gear – basically a mobile with a few Angel-friendly elements – I'll explain those in a minute – likewise a special tablet ditto. And, most importantly this wrist watch which you ought to wear permanently now. It tells the time, which I guess is no surprise. But more importantly, it is the way another Angel will get hold of you in an emergency and the way critical messages are transmitted to you."

Freddy then took about half an hour to take Andrew through the gadgets. None of the features was surprising in itself; but Andrew could now see better how it was that Angels seemed to keep so closely and quickly in touch with each other. *"With the phone and the tablet, you can now keep an eye on all the blogs around you; if you want you can easily trawl through and find exactly what it was that that the girls said about you when you first got 'acquainted' with them – though it's bad form to refer to it subsequently. But it would be my advice that you leave well alone and certainly don't go trawling in Chloe's past."* Freddy eventually ran out of things to explain. *"Just experiment and you'll quickly find your way around. Now is there anything else you need help with or answers on?"*

Andrew had a high regard for Freddy's encyclopaedic knowledge of things angelic and quickly took up the offer. *"Well, at least two things"* Andrew said. *"First, last night Michael said I had been brought into the Seraphim. Now I've heard of Cherubim and Seraphim; but what exactly is the ranking within the movement. Where do I fit in?"*

Freddy laughed but not unkindly. *"I'll give you the short version. At the top, or the centre if you'd rather, are Michael and the Archangels I told you about last time. I guess you've probably seen a bit of Gabrielle and perhaps our environmental guru but little of the others. Anyway 7 of those in all. Then nobody can be bothered with all the divisions and sub-divisions the Catholic Church used to get excited about. No 'Dominions', no 'Powers'. Instead we have an Inner Group who are called Seraphim – SCs for short, which stands for Seraphim and Cherubim – and that is amazingly what you are now. Not surprisingly there was almost no lobby wanting people called Cherubs. These SCs have greater access to Michael than us other poor mortals; you have more command over resources –*

139

someone else will provide you with a credit card and tell you what you can now spend on our behalf; it's quite a lot. That's above my pay grade. Oh, and of course, in an emergency, you can now tell me what to do."

"Right, thanks, that much I understand" said Andrew. *"Now, second question. Last night, Chloe said she didn't want to be a Watcher. What did that mean?"*

Again, Freddy smiled. *"You don't ask many easy questions do you? The short answer here is the Book of Daniel and the Book of Enoch. You'll never have heard of the latter – it's part of what's usually called the Apocrypha – the books of the Old Testament that are a bit 'iffy' in terms of their provenance. According to Enoch, Watchers were Angels who came down to Earth and were supposed to help look after the human race. However, they were male and some of them fell for human women. They bred with them and produced a race of humanoid giants – see what I mean about 'iffy'. Now again none of us have any interest in any of that. But the term 'Watcher' has come to be used for any Angel who sleeps with or gets involved with a non-Angel. There's no law against it – I know quite a few Angels who have actually gone through formal marriages with non-Angels and live with them as a married couple. But quite a few of the Angels don't want any such distractions. Chloe will have meant that she couldn't contemplate a relationship with you until you became an Angel."*

22

The next few weeks passed in a blur for Andrew. Almost without discussion, Chloe moved into his flat; and within a week, Andrew could not imagine (or, rather, did not wish to imagine) any other way of living. She, herself, seemed nearly always cheerful, certainly always calm. And the only downside of that was that she insisted on a couple of short spells a day for what she called yoga. Now, Andrew would not have called himself moody. But, like most normal people, he had mood swings; and Chloe seemed incredibly adept at sensing his mental state. She cheered him up when he needed it; she ensured that his occasional exuberance and feelings of well-being did not carry him too far. As a lover, she was beyond any woman he had ever been with before. But, more importantly in many ways, she was also his friend and a good one at that.

For Andrew, perhaps the only cloud on the horizon was that, sooner or later, she was bound to find out about the Colonel and Andrew's other life. But he consoled himself that it was only thanks to leading this double life that he had come into contact with her in the first place. And, if he imagined the worst, that there might come a time when the Colonel demanded something of him that would hurt his relations with Chloe? In that case, he had little trouble in assuring himself that the Colonel could 'go hang'. In any case, Andrew could not see that such a circumstance was particularly likely.

Andrew did raise the point with the Colonel when they next met. The Colonel had listened in silence to Andrew's description of his last labour and his acceptance into the Seraphim. He had then offered Andrew another sherry – it was early evening again – and leant back in his chair; *"I'm not likely to queer your pitch, Andrew"* he said. *"I think you've done brilliantly; and, while I shall ask you to go on reporting back, I can't see any reason why you shouldn't be able to continue meeting any obligations you may pick up as an Angel. I don't suppose it will be likely; but I really would like to meet this young lady who has so grabbed your heart. For now, though, just keep doing whatever it is that Michael or other senior Angels ask you to do; and only get in touch with me if you hear something that seems to threaten public law and order.*

And, by that, I don't mean things like your punitive expedition up to Manchester – I agree, it sounds as though the young man got less than he deserved. I mean anything that sounds like some huge public disobedience, a coup or something like that. Everything you've told me doesn't make any of that sound likely. Personally, I should be delighted if the Angels can shake up the next Election and offer some kind of alternative to the current ghastly options. "

Andrew had had no problem slipping away to see the Colonel. Chloe had made clear early on that their relationship of total trust must mean that, if it were necessary, either could say to the other *'I have to be somewhere'*. They wouldn't need to speak about it or explain themselves if they didn't want. In any case, Chloe knew he had these Middle East 'students' to train up and accepted readily that, from time to time, he would be away with them.

The weeks slipped very quickly by. Chloe seemed to have a huge range of Angel friends – Andrew wondered about the 150 limit that Michael had talked about. And both enjoyed enough of the kind of music that the Angels arranged gigs for that, several times a week, there was one – often free – they could attend in London.

Chloe's current Angel task seemed to be checking up with and reassuring a number of Angels in and around the South East. They were embedded in one or more of the social programmes – like the women's housing projects – that the Angels were increasingly majoring on. For Andrew, he received the odd request to help, the only one of which that took him away from Chloe for a few days was the need for him, after all, to go and help deliver an 'environmental special' on plastics. He did at least avoid what he heard afterwards had been a dreary few days scavenging for plastic in Bristol and around South Wales. But he did have to go down to the South Wales coast and help present – to several admiring TV anchor people – the benefits incorporated in the new plastics sorting plant.

This in turn had required several days of preparation, brushing up his schoolboy physics and getting to know his way round the small but (he was assured) extremely expensive new processing plant. The programme that resulted was an immediate and huge hit with viewers when a TV channel ran it; and, just to make sure no-one who mattered had missed it, the Angels – who Andrew discovered indeed had their own TV channel putting out about 6 hours of shows a day (mostly recorded gigs) – ran it several times on that.

Chloe had enjoyed sitting watching with him – Andrew had by default become the Angel's spokesman for the relevant interviews though Uriel had also been heavily involved. For just a few days, Andrew had become able to download chunks of erudite physics in a way that sounded both coherent and as though he had been doing it for years. For some reason, Chloe particularly enjoyed the passage where Andrew had explained the four main types of plastic and how the new process sorted between them. After a few viewings she could even recite the main text. *"There are four main types of plastic. One is PET, polyethylene terephthalate, used to make bottles for beverages. The second is High-Density polyethylene for milk bottles. A third is Polyvinyl Chloride, PVC, used in cling film; and the fourth Low Density polyethylene for grocery bags."* The first time she had done that, he had chased her around the sofa, caught her and they had fallen in a heap on the sofa kissing frantically.

Andrew regretted that his physics lessons had never been such fun.

During this period, Andrew also came to realise just how careful the Angels had been in setting up this exercise and how they pointed the way forward to what would need to be done – by implication after they had become the Government. Another passage that Andrew had learned (and, though he said so himself, he delivered very well) was a good example. *"People need to understand that over 80% of global plastic rubbish comes from Asia. We can clean up our act. But what it's really going to take is making the technology and the money available so that countries like India and Bangladesh can do this themselves; and, more importantly want to. We think China will get the message and will have the ability to do that work itself – we will just make the technology available to them. For the others, an Angel Government in the UK would be making such technology available as part of its Aid Programme. Without that, this initiative you see here today would be pretty meaningless, just like a lot of the UK Aid given in recent years has been."*

23

Not all the Angel initiatives – and there seemed to be an inexhaustible number as the months moved towards the Election – went quite so smoothly. Andrew saw one, the public pledges of political support for the Angels from leading figures, take shape and blossom. The footballer whom he had helped to cajole was just one of many from around the country, from the professions, the Arts and public life. Obviously, Andrew had no insight into how many of these were genuine statements, rather than drawn under pressure as in the case of the footballer. But most sounded heartfelt and were often backed by convincing summaries of why the individual had concluded that the present political machines were broken. They certainly seemed to achieve their purpose – of changing the public mood.

Independent journalists appeared mostly to reach a similar conclusion – that the statements were heartfelt – when they delved into some of the pledges. Likewise, press efforts to research the social programmes that the Angels had been running also failed to dig up any dirt. In fact, the opposite. By April as a result, there could have been few young mothers around the country who didn't know – and think well of – the Angel hostels for young women and families. They also knew that it was a key Angel pledge that these would be rolled out across the country if the Angels won the Election. Likewise, anyone who had ever tried dieting should by April have known that, while the Angels had no magic bullets here, they did have a programme of life change and improvement that had had a marked and lasting impact on many. And, again, that this would be tried more widely if the Angels came to power.

However, Andrew discovered too that the Angels were just as capable as anyone else of screwing up, though it wasn't common.

Somewhere, an Angel had come up with a bizarre idea for showing how mass dieting – if supported in the right way – could make a huge difference to individuals' weight and, over time, to their health and life expectancy. This Angel had started with the fact that the average female elephant weighed around 4,000 kilos. That person had also found zoo scales that allowed individual elephants to be weighed – great metal plates in the ground on which the animals could stand. And this Angel had also worked out that the various clinics like the one Andrew had been to in his second labour, for 'prize giving', were currently taking in several hundred new recruits a quarter. The Angel had obviously known about the 'secret ingredient' of diet loss – the restoration of taste buds – and wanted to show how, in an overall programme, this could work.

Andrew suspected that what followed had been dreamt up in an alcohol-fuelled evening by a group of Angels in a university. But, nevertheless, Michael had been approached and, somehow, had given the OK.

The idea was this. Take 200 recruits – male and female – who, these bright sparks had worked out, weighed around 90 kilos each on arrival. Put 10 candidates in reserve for drop-outs. The rest – the 190 – would weigh around 17,000 kilos in total, give or take – or, if you chose the right elephants – 4 adult females. The idea? Weigh both groups at the beginning of the new courses. Weigh them again at the end of the courses when many of the participants would have shed perhaps 20 kilos; and, with luck, you could find the whole 190 balanced by 3 elephants not 4. Great visual, great TV. The fact – Andrew thought – that it was in very poor taste and open to all kinds of risk in the delivery seemed to have got brushed too readily aside.

Andrew got involved only about seven weeks into the hare-brained scheme, when a message from Michael came to ask if he could take charge of the project and, if possible, save it. The idea had been launched – with one of the southern zoos providing enthusiastic support to find four female elephants and weigh them; and the same equipment had been used to weigh (in batches!) the course newcomers. Andrew quickly discovered that the

148

only good thing that could be said was that nearly all these people had been enthusiastic supporters at the outset; and they were tickled by the idea that, between them, they could lose an elephant's weight in three months. Andrew also found that almost every professional involved in dieting and weight control thought the idea was both gross and crazy. However, there would be no problem in finding doctors who would agree that the results, if maintained, would greatly improve the health and life expectancy of those involved. The stunt was now so well established in the public mind that there seemed no prospect of just quietly burying the idea and moving on; so Andrew had little choice but to make the best of it.

Andrew not surprisingly found something of a shambles on the first morning he turned up at the clinic from which the whole operation had been run. There seemed to have been no senior Angel in charge up to that point, certainly no-one who could cover the country (the clinics were spread around) or who had any real PR expertise. Andrew found it easy to take over –no-one there wanted responsibility for what was shaping up to be a disaster. And he had already taken the precaution of involving one of the central Angel team of PR experts, Georgia, with whom he had already discussed what could perhaps be done.

The first step was to organise a check on how the groups in the various clinics were actually shaping up. How many of the 190 had dropped out? The answer proved to be a very encouragingly low number; he would not need the 10 'reserves'. Then, the key question. They were nearly halfway through the course. Had the average weight of the course members fallen by anything like the 10 or so kilos per person that was going to be needed by that stage? The answer here was a little less reassuring – about 8 kilos a head from the sample that he arranged to be weighed over his first couple of days. But the good news was that nearly all of those involved claimed to be enjoying the exercise and were determined to hit their personal (and the collective) target.

Over the next month, Andrew travelled round all the clinics involved. Chloe volunteered to visit many of them with him; and he found that she had great empathy with those on the courses. This she put down to her own much earlier recovery from drug addiction on an Angel-financed course. Andrew decided that the atmosphere had to be made one of 'competitive fun'. These people had signed in to a programme, focusing on their own problems, their own need for life-style changes. Now they had found an additional element, a distinctly odd competition in which each of them could play a part.

Andrew instructed that the courses should continue as normal – i.e. there should be no extra emphasis on weight loss as opposed to the life-style change programme and the additional skill sets being taught. He guessed that, even if they met the challenge, some journalist 6 months later would track down participants and see if many of them had immediately started to regain weight at the end of the course. What the Angels knew was that the key to continued weight loss was the changes wrought in the participants' self-esteem through the addition of new life and professional skills. To skimp on these elements of the courses would be self-defeating.

Andrew also spent quite a lot of time with Georgia gaming how the final 'weigh-off' could be handled on air. The independent TV company involved had come up with that name – 'the Great Weigh-off', no doubt a play on a much earlier TV 'bake-off'; and the company was clearly intent on making it seem just that, the last round of a competition being viewed live by (they hoped) several million people.

Two days before the weigh-off, Andrew brought the 200 together. It had been agreed at the outset that the elephants themselves would not be reweighed; what they had clocked up the first time was the bar. The course members could be weighed in batches of around 50, so Andrew decided that three of those and one of 40 would be best. He also arranged some clever animation, graphics that could be shown on the TV so that, as each group was weighed, part of one of the four elephants turned from grey to red on the screen. The aim of course being to make sure that there was only one elephant left on the screen in grey when the last participants had been weighed. Andrew decided against any preparatory weighing or checking the day before the event.

Although the whole thing had been badly organised by what he had come to regard as normally high 'Angel standards', Michael had at least told him that no expense should be spared in playing it out. It needed 3 hotels in the area booked out wholly to Andrew to house the participants, a fleet of 10 coaches to transport them. And there were plenty of other costs on top. By the time the live broadcast began (at 10 a.m.) Andrew was already feeling like he had done a day's work. By the time the weighing actually started (just after 11), the only thing keeping him going was adrenaline and an odd desire to know what would happen.

The actual weighing (and the control of the computer graphics as each group was weighed) was all left in the hands of the TV company– who had made it politely but abundantly clear that anything else could be regarded by those watching as involving some form of cheating. Various 'talking heads' filled the TV hour before the weighing began, several of whom made no secret of their distaste for the exercise nor their view that any weight loss being recorded would be transient. One doctor, however, did provide balance by pointing out that, if the participants really had lost 20 kilos each and could sustain that loss, then the subsequent incidence of Type 2- diabetes in this group would be hugely reduced, while average life expectancy might have increased by at least four years. Andrew, wanting any good news, clung to those figures as he rushed around with Chloe providing last minute encouragement and support to the groups, trying to keep the atmosphere relaxed, 'fun'.

The participants themselves were individually checked by the TV company between 10 and 11, to make sure they had featured in the original weigh-in. A handful were interviewed and, to Andrew's relief, these people majored on the life skills they had been given, consigning the weight loss to an 'also-ran'.

Then the weighing, in three lots of 50 plus one of

40, took place. Most people involved seemed happy and relaxed – after all, Andrew rationalised, if they failed it would be a collective rather than an individual failure. Fortunately the weather was dry and the good humour among those participating seemed to rub off on the camera crews and the journalists who had turned up. The computer graphics had been structured, so that as a batch of 50 was weighed, the collective total was turned into 'elephant equivalent' and part of an elephant went from grey to red on the screen.

Andrew couldn't keep count of what was needed from each batch to achieve the overall target. But when the last lot, of 40 came up, he could see that nearly 2½ of the 4 elephants had turned red.

Andrew could hardly bring himself to look after the last weighing. But a ragged cheer went up from participants who, safely weighed, were standing round watching TV monitors. One whole elephant was still grey. The 190 had indeed lost around 4,000 kilos between them, the equivalent of one female elephant.

The whole thing was, as Andrew had rather hoped, a three-day wonder. But it did serve the purpose of bringing the Angels to the attention of a group of the public who probably had less idea than the average as to who the Angels were, let alone what they stood for.

The one thing Andrew did remember, from that evening, was that he and Chloe went back to his flat and he prepared a good bottle of champagne (mainly for Chloe's sake) to go with the takeaway he had ordered. He scrolled into the main Angel social site and read the now many comments from Angels who had seen or heard of the day's events but who had had no part in them. From that, he saw that he had a new nickname, 'Elephant Man'; he suspected it was going to be a long time before he shook that off!

24

Andrew spent an increasing amount of time, thereafter, helping with Angel work ahead of the Election. The Angels had in the end decided to contest nearly 400 of the 600 seats – Michael had obviously concluded that Scotland, Northern Ireland and Wales involved too much 'stretch' for them at that stage. He had also written off a number of Tory and Labour seats as 'no-hopers' first time round. The preference, clearly, had been to go for seats where Tory and Labour votes had been within about 10% of each other at the last Election and/or where there were significant numbers of Muslims and/ or younger people; or a significant vote last time for a third party (nearly always the Lib Dems).

Andrew himself knew just how much effort the Angels had put in the months up to the Election in getting Muslim and younger non-Muslim voters under 30 to sign up and ensure they could vote. Also, the organisation on the ground of the seats they were fighting seemed good. By a year before the Election, the Angels had named candidates in place for each of the constituencies they were contesting. Party offices had been rented and were up and running in most of them. All the candidates were 'local' – people who could claim reasonably close connection with the area. Also, none of them had ever been MPs before. One of the Angels' first declarations in this area had been that their proposed MPs would all be newcomers to the political scene; also that, if elected, no Angel MP would stand at more than two consecutive Elections for the same seat. Michael clearly wanted to show just how different his party was going to be from those who had dominated up to now.

Money was not in short supply, nor were ideas, many of which sought to move the new party's appeal beyond the young. Michael had once said to Andrew that the party needed at least 6-7 million votes first time round and to draw roughly half from each of the other main parties. *"Otherwise"* Michael had said *"we'll be like UKIP in 2015 – 4 million votes and just one MP. Last time, the Tories and Labour both got around 40 % of the votes cast. If we could knock 10 or 12% off both in the seats we're contesting, energise the younger voters and, in some parts of the country, appeal to Muslim and a still sizeable Lib Dem vote, we'll be getting somewhere. As soon as we get above 30% of the vote in a constituency, especially those where Tories and Labour typically both poll well, we're in the mix. And a few % on top of that will bring a large number of seats."*

With Labour that meant primarily drawing away the youth vote. For the Tories, it meant appealing to a quite different group, typically much older and more established with more to lose from a major change of Government. The typical Angel proposition here was that, after all the self-inflicted wounds over leaving Europe and with an inconsequential leader, the Tories had little chance; so why not put your vote somewhere where it might matter more and keep a left-wing Labour party out at the same time?

Andrew enjoyed the work but he found it draining. In particular, it required him to debate a lot of issues with the kind of people that the Angels needed to win over – issues which, in many cases, he had rarely thought about before. When she joined him, Chloe seemed much less affected by this; her interest in – and empathy with – sometimes dotty or inconsistent ideas struck him as amazing. But, at least for now, everything she did just made Andrew love her more and want to be with her more.

25

Over the summer, in the run –up to the Election, the pollsters usually gave the Angels 20% plus of the vote, drawn it seemed almost equally from Labour and Tory. As one of the PR people said *"Just like the Lib Dems in the good old days and a fat lot of good it did them."* One thing the Angels did take comfort from was that Angel ratings were moderately higher in the seats that they were contesting. Another 'encouragement' was that – while the Angels were stuck at this level of support, the two main parties spent most of their time and money fighting each other. Both of them obviously found it infuriating that the Angels almost totally refused to discuss Europe, the source of so much division and bitterness in both main parties over the previous decade. The basic Angel line, when pressed, had been very well put by Gabrielle (who was getting a lot of air time and favourable comment) early in the campaign. *"The UK electorate made a decision in the referendum in 2016. The country then tore itself to shreds until the final deal with the EU had been done in 2020. We have no intention of picking that deal apart. But we do hope that, by being new, by being reasonable, we can take the Agreement to a new level with active EU support, in a way that is clearly good for the UK. Until we are in power and have met with all the people here and in the EU who we shall need to talk to, that is all we can say. The subject of Europe has already done the UK enough damage."* That was a line that seemed to go down very well, especially with the younger voters.

That would probably have been that, with the Angels emulating UKIP, though – whenever Andrew got depressed – he did at least draw hope from the huge swell of optimism and purpose that he saw whenever he was with a mass of Angels. However, over the last two weeks of the campaign, things changed, with three 'surprises' (the term afterwards coined by political journalists who had been wrong-footed).

The first came just 12 days before the Election. Clearly Michael and others had been working on it for some time and, to some extent, must have influenced the timing. However it had panned out, the result was that, over a 24 hour period, based on information provided by the Angels but especially by the Muslim Angels, a major terrorist cell that seemed ready to launch a wave of attacks was smashed by police, in the Midlands and in London. The police themselves were a little coy about how they had been given such productive and 'live' leads; but Jibril wasn't. And he had such detail at his fingertips that, within another 24 hours, the police were admitting off the record that they had been led to the main addresses and given a vast amount of prior information by the Angels.

Michael's PR people played this cleverly. Of course, it had been vital to tell the police now before the attacks had been launched – it was the proximity of these attacks that had determined that the time had come to spring the trap. But this was not just a 'dividend' from having the Angels actively around; it was – the Angel PR machine implied – just a first instalment on what could be expected in future. 'Undercover' Angels – mostly Muslim – had come up with the information and passed it on, often at great personal risk.

The second 'surprise' was similar in its way. Just a couple of days later, police were able to intercept large drug hauls in Edinburgh and Liverpool. And this time, Angels who had once themselves been addicts had come forward with information that would put the rings concerned away for years. Even though, in a few cases, individual Angels were themselves going to have to admit to offences that would involve prison sentences. As Gabrielle said in an early interview after the news had broken: *"Any drug lord anywhere in this country now knows that he may have people working for him who actually belong to us. And that these people are now brave enough – because they have Angel resources behind them – to stand up and be counted."*

When Andrew first heard of the drug busts, his initial reaction was to shrug his shoulders. Drugs were now so widespread and varied that even a couple of major seizures were just small waves on a big ocean. But, over the next couple of days, as the press took on board both these 'surprises', Andrew had to admit that they were playing very well with a critical part of the Electorate, the older and richer who seemed to take such threats to their wellbeing the most seriously.

26

Neither of these 'surprises' by themselves in the common view afterwards would have been enough to swing a huge number of votes towards the Angels. But, when the third happened, the three together had an enormous effect.

It was the Saturday before the Election, so just five days to go. The Angels had organised a variety of events, several of which of course were music festivals, around the country. But one of these had been set up as a gig in the Park, the Park being Hyde Park. That location had been the stage for a number of big music events over the years. But somehow Michael had got approval for a twist at the beginning. Michael himself would fly in by helicopter, make a short speech to rally the troops and then leave the 150,000 or so expected to enjoy some of the best bands in the country. Most of these bands, Andrew later found, had contributed their services for free. The tickets themselves cost a ludicrously cheap £10. But even that was enough to pay for the remaining expenses, thus avoiding any risk of the Angels being accused of spending that should have been counted as part of their 'allowance' under the rules governing Election spending.

Perhaps more difficult must have been getting official approval for the helicopter to come in; but Michael had obviously called in a few favours; and probably the London authorities didn't want to appear in any way to be blocking the Election hopes of a party that, anyway, wasn't contesting many London seats.

Andrew and Chloe had been lined up to be among the 1,000 or so Angel stewards needed to run the event – something that Chloe at least had done several times before. When they went to the rehearsal the day before, they were told that they should position themselves by 10 a.m. near the front of the main music stage. Michael's helicopter would fly in; he would walk about 100 yards along a prepared turf path, make a short address and then leave, to move onto the next rally. As they would be sharing this space with the Angels' Choir who would be providing the pre-show entertainment, that sounded pretty easy. And Andrew had heard the Choir before and knew how good they were. Most of the music they sang had a religious background. The first time Andrew had heard them singing a version of some Taize chants in Latin and English, he had actually felt deeply stirred, most unusual for him.

By 10 a.m. on the day, Andrew and Chloe were on parade as requested. It was a cool crisp autumn day but mercifully there was no sign of rain. Andrew reflected, not for the first time, how lucky the Angels seemed to be with regard to the weather for their big outdoor events. Proceedings were meant to start around 12, with Michael's arrival. The music was expected to carry on until late evening and end with a candle-light vigil/ celebration; and Andrew quickly heard from several around him, the word was that Michael would return to lead the closing ceremony.

By noon, there were at least 80,000 of the expected 150,000 present and the wide array of food and drink tents and vans were doing a roaring trade. He had got Chloe and himself a couple of coffees about 10.30 – the coffee not as good as he was now used to at Angel events but still very welcome in the circumstances.

Around 11.30 the Choir started up and ran initially with songs that were well known and could be sung along to. Within minutes, the Choir had got several thousand new and untrained members. But, while to Andrew's ear, it didn't sound that good, it was certainly helping to create the right kind of atmosphere. Just once Andrew smelled smoke indicating that others there were getting mellow with chemicals. But he knew better than to go charging around looking for the source and remonstrating. The Angel approach was typically to acknowledge but ignore the existence of recreational drugs, just as with alcohol. Indeed, in his near year with the Angels now, Andrew could not remember ever seeing an Angel drunk or under the influence of drugs.

Just after 12, a helicopter flew in low above the stage and set itself down about 100 yards away. The giant TV screens – which were later going to enable most of the crowd to actually see what was going on, on stage – swung round towards the craft. But the operators were clearly a long way away –i.e. near the stage – and the pictures weren't in very sharp focus anyway.

The helicopter door opened and a metal stairway quickly rolled up to it. What happened then became some of the most contested (and watched-over) TV footage in history, especially the material shot by the main TV camera crews who were trained on the helicopter. Andrew himself wasn't watching the screens. He was busy making sure that the barrier marking out the walkway up to the stage was clear, that the crowds starting to press round it were far enough away; and that there were enough stewards around to provide an outer circle of protection for Michael as he walked to the Stage. (Over-enthusiastic Angel supporters wanting to touch Michael or, worse, grab a piece of his clothing were a well-known phenomenon that Andrew had been told very clearly needed to be avoided now.) Everything, he had been told, needed to look good on TV. For every person present here, there would probably be 10 people watching at home; and, if you counted in those who would later watch the news headlines, that number probably rose from 10 to 40.

What happened next, Andrew was only able to piece together after the event. What seemed to happen was that a number of Michael's entourage appeared at the top of the helicopter steps and descended, waiting to surround

Michael when he came down. Andrew had already seen that there were a slew of foreign and domestic Press and TV people milling around, in a pen to which they had been admitted only after the helicopter had touched down. 'Health and Safety in action even here' he had thought at the time.

Then a figure in white appeared at the top of the steps and raised both hands in greeting. The crowd – most of whom were at least 100 yards away – greeted this with a growing chorus of welcome, as they picked it up on the large monitors round the stage. Several groups of Angels started chanting Michael's name – something which, again, Andrew had seen and heard several times before.

And then?

All Andrew **heard** was a short burst of gunfire. Everyone afterwards argued about the number of shots. But Andrew had at least trained with and under gunfire in the Army, so he had more faith in his own recollections than what Chloe or others told him afterwards. He heard 3 shots in very quick succession. When he turned to look at the big monitors, the figure at the top of the steps had collapsed. The next 20 seconds seemed like an eternity; but he checked afterwards, 20 seconds was all it had taken for someone (he thought Gabrielle who had already descended) to shout *"Get him away, back in the chopper; get him away from here."* Gabrielle and several of her companions raced back up the steps; 3 of the men bent over the slumped figure and, with Gabrielle's help, each took an arm or a leg and bundled him back into the helicopter. The door then shut, the rotors started up – they had barely ceased rotating after landing a minute earlier – and about 45 seconds later the helicopter lurched into the sky and was gone.

Around Andrew, it was pandemonium. Roughly half those around him there were turning to flee, clearly having been terrified by the gunshots and fearing more. The other half – including nearly all the Angels themselves were already running towards the scene of the shooting, some in silence, others screaming in anger. Among the photographers themselves there was equal disorder. A few had flung themselves on one of their number and were pinning him to the ground. The few police around were moving in on that group. From their starting point 100 yards away, angry Angels were now arriving outside the photo pen. And it didn't take a great mind to foresee that something very nasty might be about to happen to the individual on the ground.

That this didn't happen was the serendipitous combination of two things. First, there must have been a senior officer among the police; and by the time the helicopter had taken off, she had detailed the men with her to surround the struggling pile of humanity on the ground. Second, most of the TV crews themselves had decided that it was their job – and probably a lot safer – to record these events for posterity; and a rough ring of cameras had, in that same time, surrounded the police cordon. Such is the deference which people now show to cameras that, by the time the first groups of angry Angels had arrived, this twin cordon was established; and it soon became apparent that the arrivals would take things no further.

27

Andrew remembered little of the next few hours. Chloe had had hysterics and nothing Andrew could do seemed to help much. Within about 20 minutes of the shooting, large extra numbers of police had turned up and at least one person from the pack of photographers had been hurried away. The police then systematically began clearing the area, starting at the photographers' pen. Andrew, as one of the more senior Angels present, was able to round up 100 or so Angel stewards who, under police direction, helped get people away.

Eventually, about 4 p.m. the police and a few Angels were the only ones left in the area. Andrew decided he had to get Chloe out and back somewhere safe. His flat was the only place he could think of. But, as he was doing that, his Angel watch vibrated and a light came on indicating an urgent message. This said merely 'Be at Higham Hall in Hertfordshire by 10 a.m. tomorrow. Come tonight if you can, food and beds available. Gabrielle.'

Andrew checked that Chloe's watch had produced the same message; it had. Now there was, at least, something they could do, Andrew eventually managed to calm Chloe down a little and tell her they had to get back to his flat, take his car and get to wherever Higham Hall was.

Afterwards, Andrew always found it distasteful to recall any detail from the hours that followed. Chloe did as she was told but looked and acted like a doll whose stuffing had been completely knocked out of it. Andrew pretty well dragged her out of Hyde Park, found a taxi within a couple of hundred yards and bundled her in.

Even the taxi driver had caught the mood around the area. As Andrew settled her on the back seat, the driver relayed the information that the police were apparently holding several people for questioning; but that nothing else was known. The rumour mill and the conspiracy theorists, however, were already in full cry.

Somehow, Andrew got Chloe back to his flat. He packed a bag for himself and one for her – she was now effectively living with him, so that was easy. They watched the early evening news bulletin, which led with 'Party leader shot at rally' and reprised the relatively limited footage that the news channel had managed to acquire. Nothing new. He got Chloe down to his car and, having set his satnav, headed off through North

London. Chloe just lay in the passenger seat behind him, crying when she had the energy, but otherwise relapsing into awful, ominous, silence before bursting out again. Andrew quickly decided there was nothing he could do or say that would make any difference, though he also knew he would never forget these awful few hours.

With the satnav, Higham Hall proved easy enough to find. They arrived about 8 p.m. and were bundled in. Chloe was immediately taken off by friendly female hands, some of the women obviously knew her well. Andrew was taken for some food – hot soup, bread and cheese, after it had been quickly established that he was in a fit state to help others and didn't need the help himself. Roughly half the Angels who had already got there were sufficiently in control of their emotions to work, helping the Sisters who had been there from the start. Andrew spent most of his time up until midnight meeting late arrivals, sorting out the ones who most needed help and enlisting the others to help. Part of the time, he found himself in the kitchens – Heaven knows how the Sisters had coped with this totally unexpected influx of grieving humanity. But tinned soup and bread seemed to be in endless supply; and, as the evening went on, a few bottles of spirit found round the place got very short shrift.

When he finally collapsed onto a small mound of bedding around 1 a.m., he guessed perhaps 300 Angels had got there. By common consent, no-one spoke about the day's events, save sometimes to hug someone near them and, more often than not, burst into tears. Andrew's Army training left him a little better able to function than many; but when he did have five minutes to reflect to himself, he felt a sick hopelessness that he guessed was what was being felt all around him.

28

Higham Hall had been built in the days of innumerable country weekends and elaborate entertainment. Even with 300 unexpected guests, there was room once some of the outbuildings had been reconnoitred and declared fit for sleeping. Several of the Sisters seemed to know the estate well, so Andrew guessed the Angels must have used it before.

As people awoke the next morning, they were chivvied into groups and provided with what breakfast was available – certainly with lots of hot drinks and a great deal of cereal. Andrew guessed – rightly it later turned out – that all the local Balden stores had been emptied on Saturday evening, to make this possible.

It also became clear quickly that a large number of journalists and TV hacks had been invited too, though they had all been told to get there on Sunday morning. The Hall held a huge ballroom; and that is where the journalists were put as they arrived. Some Angel group had clearly been at work there. One end of the ballroom had been cut off by a theatre curtain – in its heyday Higham had played host to a number of small plays on the stage that lay behind the curtain, so maybe this had already been there. The stage itself jutted out just a little beyond the curtains and, in the centre of that visible flooring, there was just a free-standing mike.

The invitees gathered on the main floor. He could see a lot of Angels, including a number he knew. But, whoever was organising the Angels today, clearly they did not need him. Most of those he saw and knew, not surprisingly, were keeping to themselves and looking thoroughly downcast. Most of the media arrivals looked like their attendance had been settled by the relevant editor or producer only that morning; and some looked like they either hadn't been to bed on the Saturday night or had only recently been hauled out of that bed to attend. Certainly what coffee and pastries there were took a hammering, especially given that, at mid-morning, even hardened journalists would have been surprised to find alcohol available.

Andrew had got one of the girls to find Chloe, help her dress and bring her to him. She was better than the previous night but totally withdrawn. He found her a cup of coffee and did his best with her. But what could he say that might be of any use? All he could think of was to point her towards the announcement that presumably Gabrielle was going to make. *"We have to stay strong"* he urged Chloe *"Michael wouldn't have wanted anything else".*

Like him, the few people he did talk to thought that some kind of statement would be forthcoming from Gabrielle; and it would depend on that what happened next. Would she take on the leadership? Presumably so. Would they go on contesting the Election? Who knew?

Andrew listened to some of the journalists' conversations around him and sought to catch up on the news. There was little hard news. Apparently, the police were not yet willing to say whether there had been one assassin or more, or whether the one man they did have in custody was the one who had fired the shots. Many of these journalists were fierce rivals, or at least their papers were. But there was – he had seen before – also a grudging camaraderie among them. So, Andrew overheard several shared stories about how X had been rung by his editor at 10 the previous evening and told to haul his butt over here by 10 am Sunday – or else. It turned out the one good thing the shortage of time had meant was that one of the TV camera crews was being paid to provide photographs as needed for all, so the press people had for the most part been able to leave their own photographers behind. When the conversations strayed onto why they were here, Andrew could establish that – like himself – the media could see no reason why they were there other than the one he had come up with. And most of those media obviously felt it was a pretty poor reward for a ruined Saturday night and no lie-in on a Sunday morning.

As 11 a.m. approached, the noise in the room and the apprehension that was swirling around, unseen but felt by all, rose several notches. The Angels were known for sticking to pre-set timetables though this of course was an unprecedented occasion. But by 11 a.m. itself, the camera crews were in place and most of the individuals had edged to somewhere that they thought would give adequate view of whatever was to happen. Andrew realised that no chairs had been put out – whatever this was, it was clearly going to be short if not sweet.

At 11 precisely, Gabrielle stepped out from behind the curtain and, with the mike on, called for attention. She got it within 10 seconds. No doubt the visitors were as interested as Andrew was to find out what was happening.

Gabrielle was wearing a long plain flowing dress, interestingly with no outward sign of mourning. She looked like what she was, the Number 2 of a large and important organisation. Like nearly all the Angels Andrew had met, she radiated self-confidence and inner calm. Nearly all those present would know who she was; so Gabrielle made no self-introduction but launched straight into what she had to say.

"I want to thank all of you for coming at such short notice. I promise you, though, that whatever you are currently thinking, you will within 20 minutes be glad that you made the effort. Within the hour you will be downloading a great story, an almost miraculous story, to your readers and listeners. Indeed, I can imagine many of you are already poised on social media to spread whatever that story is; though I must warn (and apologise for the fact) that – until we have finished – the jamming devices we have

here will mean that none of your output – even the TV feeds – will be going anywhere. We want you to hear and understand before you communicate.

Enough prelude. The past is easy to describe. Around mid-day yesterday, three shots (we think) were fired at a man about to walk down the steps of a helicopter in Hyde Park. He was hit, he collapsed and, as our own internal procedures have always provided for in the case of such an awful event, those surrounding him bundled him up and back into the helicopter. In case there should be further shots or more trouble. The helicopter took off; and then there was almost complete radio silence from us until the messages that went out from here last night calling you in today.

Gabrielle paused and looked around. She certainly had the audience's attention though they were almost radiating incomprehension. She continued.

"The man who was about to walk down those helicopter steps was – tragically for him, wonderfully for us – NOT Michael. His name was Adrian Cowley and, in a short while, you will be able to see his body and the bullet marks on him. You will see that he bears more than a passing resemblance to Michael, though those of us who know Michael would never have been fooled for more than a minute. When you have seen Adrian, we will be handing his body over to the police, as well of course as making ourselves available to them.

I now need to explain how this came about. The day before the concert, we received word from the intelligence authorities of rumours of a planned attack on Michael. This is not the first time we have had such warnings; up to now all had been false alarms.

We didn't want to do what the authorities would have liked – which was to call off the concert or, at least, for Michael

176

not to go. But this latest warning had more 'legs' than previous rumours. So, what to do?

The authorities thought that the arrival by helicopter would be the point at which any assassin would likely strike. The front rows to the stage where Michael would be speaking from were already set significantly well back; and the expected occupants of those first seats were all known and pre-vetted. The opportunities for an assailant there would be very limited.

After much debate among ourselves and with the authorities, Michael agreed that someone would stand in for him in walking from the helicopter to the dais. The idea was concocted that this person would get to the stage and immediately introduce the 'real' Michael who would be sitting directly in front of the stage. The explanation would be that we need to remind people that we must all avoid preconceptions. We wanted to warn that now, and in the future, people – and by that we particularly mean voters next week – need to be sure that they are getting the right message from the right source. He would highlight this by pointing out just how many people there would have been shouting for him just a few minutes earlier, when actually they had been hailing a complete stranger.

Now, the authorities offered to find someone to impersonate Michael. But, as some of you will know, Michael is surrounded by people who love him deeply, many of whom have been with him for years. One of these, Adrian Cowley, insisted that he would stand in for Michael. Indeed, he pointed out that this would not be the first time that people had actually mistaken him for Michael in real life. He would not be budged. In the end, Michael agreed.

You may well think this ruse was fraught with danger and that, if it had gone ahead as planned, would have appeared as a not very clever party trick. But we were stuck between a rock – the rumour of an attack – and a hard place, not wanting to deprive so many loyal supporters of a last chance to see Michael before the Election.

Tragically, Adrian paid the ultimate price; but, I stress, it would otherwise have been Michael himself. When the shots rang out and Adrian had obviously been hit, Michael and his two helpers immediately faded into the crowd, much of which – you will recall – was by then already surging angrily towards the man who we think fired the shots. So all that really required was for Michael and the helpers to move slowly away from the scene, as others surged towards the action. In a minute we will be showing you TV footage taken at the time by our own Angel cameraman, who had of course been let into the secret of what was intended, so that he could pick out Michael at the right time.

Why didn't Michael stay? Why haven't we said anything before this morning? Well, simply because Michael and I decided, as soon as we spoke to each other, that the assassination attempt could well be part of a wider, unfinished, plot. For all we knew, there were other would-be assassins around to finish the job. We wanted a little time – and at least the initial investigations of the Metropolitan Police – to make as sure as we can that Michael would be safe when we revealed what had happened. In the meantime, it would be no bad thing if the killer or killers thought their efforts had succeeded. I apologise now to any of you who came this morning who got grilled by Security as you came in. I should also tell you we have hidden official marksmen round you right now. We will not willingly run risks in future. We think Michael is safe; but we are going to make sure that Adrian's death is not wholly in vain."

At this point, a curtain on the wall behind Gabrielle opened to reveal a huge TV screen. *"We have edited what you are about to see, to show the whole event. But I can assure any doubters among you that, later, anyone can have access to all the TV footage we have."*

The screen sprang into life, split into two. The audience then watched mesmerised and in almost complete silence while events unfolded. On the left screen, the camera picked out what now looked obviously to be Michael sitting quietly in the front row of the VIP seats immediately in front of the dais. On the right, the camera showed the helicopter landing, 'Michael' i.e. Adrian getting out and about to walk down the steps, the shots ringing out, the body falling. Then the sudden freeze that had hit the scene – followed by those around the fallen 'Michael' scooping him up between four of them, getting back into the helicopter which then took off. As these events materialised, the left hand screen showed the look of surprise and horror on the face of the real Michael, his putting a hand on each of his companions and then the three of them rising to slip away in the confusion and hubbub that had already surrounded them.

The presentation ended and Gabrielle slipped from the stage, almost unseen. It stood bare for a few seconds, then the lights over it shone even brighter. And, to a barely heard but physically felt collective intake of breath, Michael walked out on the stage and seized the microphone.

"I shall play over in my mind the events of yesterday again and again...... If I could go back in time to noon yesterday, I would willingly have exchanged my place with Adrian and let the assassin do his work. But I can't and we now have, lying

in the next room as you can see shortly, the first Angel martyr. I pray that he will remain the only one. I can only draw comfort from the fact that I have known Adrian for years and, long ago, established that his commitment to our cause was as great as mine. What he would say if he were here and what I say to you now is – as John Major might once have put it – 'don't let the bastards win'.

Lift your heads. We must take what we can from this disaster. The Angels have begun a political movement that is intended to reshape and mend our broken country. The next step for that movement is to triumph in the General Election on Thursday. Whatever the police enquiry finally shows – whether this killing was the act of a lone madman or a conspiracy, whether it was from extreme Left or Right – it is our task to move forward and start what will be a long and painful process of regrowth.

That is enough from me. Indeed, I don't think I could bear to say more. The media is welcome to view and photograph Adrian's body, though please respect him. I will then circulate among you so that those of you who know me, which I think will be at least half of you, can reassure themselves that it is indeed me. Between now and Wednesday evening, I will be flying round the country, appearing in as many major towns as I can and where the police can provide adequate security cover; and I will be speaking to reassure people. What has happened is a tragedy, though some of the Angels may think of it quite wrongly as a miracle. This is a tragedy – be in no doubt – in which a really good man gave his life unwittingly. On Thursday and from then on, let us make sure his sacrifice counts for something good."

Michael walked from the Stage. The audience, which until then had largely been silent, erupted. Angels were

180

hugging and kissing each other. Chloe, who had been standing near Andrew, quickly found him and hugged him so hard he feared for his ribs. *"The best day of my life"* she said. *"I have Michael again and I have you. I'll never let either of you go."*

29

ndrew and Chloe made their way back to London as quickly as they could, held up only by the fact that the scenes at Higham Hall after Michael had spoken were chaotic. Chloe was transformed. Laughing at anything remotely pleasing and just buzzing again with the life and verve he had come to regard as normal for her.

Chloe spent much of her time on the way back to London sending messages to her Angel circle. After all, Andrew realised, only about 300 Angels had actually been present at Higham. And, despite the fact that the story would now be going out on every possible news media, he realised that an Angel – who like Chloe – could say 'I was there, I saw Michael' would bring great comfort to her friends, now of course his friends too.

For his own part, Andrew thought long and hard about what to do next. There were two actions that now seemed unavoidable, though the thought of the second filled him with dread. At least, he could comfort himself, the order of these two actions was very clear; and the less threatening one had to be done first.

Andrew had never used it before. But, on getting back to his flat, Andrew rang the telephone number, the 'get out of jail card' which the Colonel had given him. The circumstances were not those for which the number had been designated; but Andrew felt it was vital that he now confronted the Colonel and he knew no other way of getting this done really quickly.

The voice at the end of the phone listened without comment to Andrew's message, which was that the Colonel must get in touch with him immediately. And, amazingly, within the hour, Andrew's mobile rang and the Colonel was on the line.

"My boy" said the Colonel *"I was thinking of giving you a ring. Our favourite Sheik has just given the UK a splendid military order, largely to show his gratitude for what you and we have done for him on the money laundering front. It occurred to me that a small celebration with you would be in order; and I guess, from the briefing I've just had about Higham Hall that you wouldn't object to a celebration either. Now, the FCO won't pay for it. But if you come to my Club – say around 7 tonight – we could have dinner. It's one of the few places open in central London on a Sunday night where the food is reasonable. We can have a drink over the deal; and you can tell me whatever it is that you're bursting to let me know."*

Andrew established that, as he would have expected, the Club concerned was in Pall Mall and would be littered with tributes to the British military of a former age. *"That will suit very well, Colonel. I'll see you there."*

Chloe was quite happy to be left to her own devices – indeed, she had been on the phone or internet almost continuously for about three hours now and would probably not have noticed for some time had Andrew just quietly left the flat without telling her. By just after 7, Andrew and the Colonel were seated at the latter's favourite table at his favourite club. The Colonel was recommending that the roast would be particularly good on a Sunday and promised Andrew a suitably good burgundy to wash it down.

The orders given, the two sat silently and looked at each other. The dining room – this was a Sunday night after all – was almost deserted, so there was no danger of their being overheard. When the wine came and had been poured, the Colonel broke the silence, raised his glass to Andrew and said *"Well, there are several thousand workers up North who will have a job for the next few years thanks to you. The Sheik was particularly grateful for your rapid assistance on the money-laundering front; and, like most of his kind, he worries night and day about how to limit the military threat from Iran just over the horizon. A happy conjunction of circumstances.*

Now, I understand from my contacts that you may have been at Higham Hall this morning so I guess you might anyway be in celebratory mood tonight. What I can't quite work out is why you are so desperate to see me, so desperate as to misuse that phone number I drummed into you. Do you want to cover that, so that we can then just sit back and enjoy the evening?"

"Fine by me" replied Andrew, who – over the last hour or so – had been mulling over different lines by

which he could approach what was on his mind. *"It's quite simple, really. I just want to know whether you or any of your numerous and shadowy colleagues had anything to do with the attack on Michael. I am now an Angel. And that's much more important to me than being one of your bagboys. It's partly because of my girl, Chloe. But I have also, to my slight surprise, found myself buying more and more firmly into the whole Angel story.*

I'm afraid to say that one of the thoughts I had just seconds after the awful events at Hyde Park yesterday was that you or one of yours had decided to intervene. Probably because the Angels are doing 'too well' in Election terms; because some of the powers that be are getting concerned that control could suddenly drain from their hands into the almost completely unknown and untried hands of the Angels.

I should also admit that, later, I wondered if, in fact you and yours had pulled a much more sophisticated trick with quite a different aim. You probably provided the warning to the Angels about the assassination. You would or should have known about the 'switch' from Michael to this man Cowley. Perhaps you arranged for Cowley's death, to make Michael feel obligated to you and dependent on you for information. You, after all, would have been shown to be right, in forecasting an attack. It would certainly have been relatively easy for you to find some nut, arm him and make it possible for him to get in among the photographers.

I'm sorry to be so untrusting. And, indeed, if I were being fully logical, I wouldn't be here now asking you what happened, as you would lie your head off – if you had been involved. Maybe I'm just too trusting. But I did feel I had to see you and hear, for myself, whether what you say has the ring of truth about it."

The Colonel didn't seem put out by Andrew's outburst. *"It's certainly true"* he replied *"that I have lived most of my life in an environment where truth can be a rare commodity. And I can't swear to you now that absolutely everything you have said is nonsense. I hold a senior position in the intelligence services; but, as you'll appreciate, even I won't get told everything.*

That said, I can confirm that, yes, it was my people who warned the Angels about the possibility of an attack. And, yes, we did know about the likely switch of personnel. But that's all. We are not accustomed to putting our operatives in a situation like this wretched loner found himself (if that is indeed what he was). We wouldn't have let one of our operatives undertake a mission where he was bound to be caught. And, if he had been a loner we were using for our own ends, we would certainly have made sure that he didn't live long enough to be captured and questioned.

There certainly will be an internal inquiry into why we didn't do better in seeing things coming. But, believe me, we are in this case – and very appropriately – on the side of the angels. It was our marksmen spread round Higham Hall earlier today, to keep Michael safe. It is us who will be keeping him safe as he hops around the country for the next few days."

The Colonel stopped. *"Finally, Andrew – and you are the first person to whom I am admitting this – it is the case that from Friday – whatever the result of the Election – I shall be in a new job. As the Head of Security for the Angels, for Michael personally. I too am an Angel at heart, though not yet one openly. I can understand only too well the road you have been travelling, which is one that I have been travelling covertly for a long time. I just hope this is enough to reassure you that your concerns over 'me and mine' are without foundation."*

186

30

Andrew left the Colonel's club in better spirits than when he had arrived. He **had** felt that The Colonel's arguments had made sense; and he had been hugely surprised but delighted to find that the Colonel would soon be declaring his support for the Angels by joining them. One of the two weights on his mind had eased. Which just left the second, the one he was really frightened about.

All the way through life, he had adopted the approach that, if there was some major hurdle to overcome, then it made sense not to wait around but, for better or worse, try and jump it. So, when he got home and found Chloe still up and still bubbling, he decided that there would be no better time than now to level with her. If he did not but tried to keep his secret, he knew that one day somehow it would come out. If Chloe were going to accept what he had to say, there could be no better time than now to say it; and no better person than him to own up.

He got Chloe to sit down and poured two large glasses of wine for them. *"Now, I need to talk to you"* he said. *"Let me just say what I have to say and then, only then, tell me what you honestly feel." "Sounds ominous"* Chloe replied. *"I hope you haven't been with a girl tonight and want to tell me the bad news now."*

"No" replied Andrew *"It's much more serious than that, at least it is to me. And, until you know about it and hopefully can forgive me, I shall get no rest. There is a giant shadow over our relationship which I need to disperse once and for all.*

Where to start? Well, you know I came out of the Army about 5 years ago and you know that I've been working for a megabank since then. That, of course, is all true. What you don't know is that, when I left the Army, I stayed in one important sense, by agreeing to be a 'sleeping asset' for one of the security services. I have actually only done a couple of jobs for them in the last 5 years and nothing too stressful or dangerous. In return, apart from paying me a bit of money, they have helped boost my career a bit. The arrangement has suited me well.

To move on, over a year ago now, my handler – who I've been to see tonight by the way – asked me to get involved with the Angels. He wanted me to find out what you guys were really up to, I suppose. That was why I turned up at that Oxford Street store where we first met and what, initially, drove me to get involved.

Cutting a long story short, two things subsequently happened and I can't really say what order they happened in. One was that the more I came to see of the Angels, the more I felt aligned with their aims. The other was to fall hopelessly and irrevocably in love with you.

Until the supposed assassination, I guess I'd never thought seriously about what would happen if, for any reason, my attachment to the Angels and my love for you were conflicted. But the hours after Hyde Park, I realised two things. First, faced with the need to make a choice, I would always and without a second thought choose you over the Angels. Though that doesn't mean I am not a serious believer in what they aim to do. The second realisation was that, until you knew about how our paths had met and understood what had happened to me since, our relationship would always be under a cloud. I would always worry that you'd find out somehow and that you wouldn't understand."

Chloe lifted her wine glass and took a large mouthful. *"Is that it? No secret lover, nothing else to tell me?"* Andrew just shook his head, not daring to say anything; this was the pivotal moment. *"Well, I think – if you had asked me to guess 5 minutes ago what you were about to say – that what you have actually said wouldn't have been on my guess list. That said, I can't claim that it gives me any problems at all. I have had plenty of chances recently to see and feel that you love me, that this is not all some show you've put on. I believe you whole-heartedly. As for the little subterfuge you've been hiding with, I have to think back to my own past – and not just the time when I was drug-dependent and down for the count. I did lots of things then that I'm not proud about; I've never told you about them and you've been the perfect gentleman and not asked. Perhaps I should have told you, perhaps I should now. But I know that, just like your love for me, the love I have for you 'now' is real; and I certainly hope that what you think of me wouldn't be changed one iota if you did know all my grizzly past.*

In short, I'm glad you told me. It doesn't make any difference to me. You'll have to do much more than that to get rid of me!"

31

Five days later, Andrew and Chloe lay on the double bed, fully dressed. The adrenaline had kept them going through Election Day and until about 9 a.m. on the Friday. By then, they had seen enough to know that the Angels would narrowly be the single largest party in the new Parliament, though – of course given their patchy contesting of constituencies – not a majority. Once that had become clear and, after hugging it seemed every member of the Campaign Team, they had gone across the road to their hotel and collapsed. For Andrew about four hours sleep had been enough. Now, at about 3.30, he was awake again and had been for some time.

Chloe was still fast asleep, snoring lightly as she often did. Andrew had always actually enjoyed that noise, provided he wasn't himself desperate for sleep; and he looked down now, benignly, at her – enjoying this evidence of her vulnerability and marvelling that anyone could look so beautiful while sprawled across a bed.

The last few days had passed in a dream. After Michael's seemingly miraculous reappearance, the atmosphere at Higham Hall had been close to euphoric. Michael had urged his supporters to remember that someone special to him (and now to the Angels) had died. But, try as they might, neither Andrew nor Chloe could keep the wonder and joy out of their voices and hearts. Their lives had seemingly been snatched away and then given back. Now, Andrew had faced up to his two demons; the Colonel was innocent and Chloe knew about his past but still loved him.

Most of Monday was given over to continued communication with their Angel friends – after all, they had been two of only perhaps 300 Angels who had been at Higham. They were asked the same questions over and again: 'What really happened?' 'Are you sure it was Michael?' And, less often 'What do we do now?'

The media of course had had a field day; and there had even been suggestions from some quarters that the Election should be postponed, at least until more was known about the attack and its source. But, when people realised that might well mean waiting months if not years, that suggestion quickly fell away.

The pollsters, after the Election, thought that – had the Election been held just 24 or 48 hours earlier, the Angels might have been elected in a landslide. As it was, they still benefitted hugely – from the publicity, from Michael's apparent amazing good fortune and also by the mature way he handled the events.

Now, Andrew picked up the TV remote and put one of the main Channels on, very softly. By 3, the TV talking heads had run out of energy and ideas. Andrew guessed that most of them had come onto the programme early that morning. But they would have been up most of the night, to follow events so that they could comment sensibly the next day. They were exhausted, like him.

Once it had become apparent that no Party was anywhere near being able to form a majority Government, these supposed experts had been able only to speculate without any real knowledge about what the Angels might do with the 200 seats they looked like ending up with. As the Tories and Labour had 160 and 150 seats respectively, either could in theory join with the Angels to form a majority in Parliament. The others – SNP 40, the Liberal Democrats 25, the various Irish 15, the rest (Plaid Cymru, the Greens etc) 10 – were not big enough by themselves to make much odds.

What had been clear in the run up to the Election was that none of the established parties had ever given a moment's thought to the Angels as a properly established political force. The common assumption had been that, like UKIP a few years before, the Angels might poll a lot of votes and end up with virtually no seats. Also, mud had been slung at the Angels from both sides; and there would have to be a great deal of humble pie eaten by any party that now intended to go into coalition with them.

About the only thing the experts could agree on was now that a Labour-Tory pact was impossible, while, without the Angels, neither Tory nor Labour could create a workable coalition.

The experts were put out of their misery when, about 3.40, Michael called a press conference for 4.15. Andrew guessed it would be at the Methodist Hall at Westminster and, for a minute, wondered if he should rouse Chloe and go. However, he realised quickly that this would be a waste of time – even if they could get there by 4.15 and even if they could get in.

Now that the talking heads had a time target, the TV discussion turned to what sort of conditions Michael might demand for a deal with either main party. It was politics as usual as far as these people were concerned. Would there, for example, need to be a written agreement as the Lib Dems had insisted on with their 2010 pact with the Tories?

At exactly 4.15 the cameras moved to the conference. They focused on a wide, empty, but well-lit stage – yes, it had to be the Methodist Hall, Andrew thought. At 4.17 Michael himself walked alone from the wings and went to a central podium. There was a hum of excited chatter round the Hall, only stilled as Michael held up a hand and spoke.

"I have called this gathering to do three things" he said. Not for the first time, Andrew marvelled at how Michael could seem so calm and untouched by the events of the last few days. No sign of a man who had nearly been killed, who had watched and waited Election night with them all, and could not have had more than a couple of

hours of sleep. *"First, I want to thank the people of Britain for the massive vote of confidence you have given us. Over 6 million people voted for us even though in many parts of the UK there was no Angel candidate that you could vote for. We take huge comfort from your endorsement of us; and I promise that we will not let you down. We will not return to the politics as usual that you have so resolutely turned your backs on.*

Second, I want to record publicly my heartfelt thanks to the thousands of supporters without whose staggering efforts in the last few weeks, this success would not have been possible. I will have much more to say to you over the days and weeks ahead. But know now that I will never forget.

Third – and it really harks back to the first of my commitments – I want to say something about how we intend to go forward. There is and can be no question of our reaching an accord, doing a deal, with any of the other parties. By fielding 600 candidates, both the Tories and Labour polled many more total votes than we did. But it is hard to deny the facts – only one party, ours, comes out of this Election with any kind of mandate.

For us to engineer a coalition would be politics as usual; it would be a slap in the face for the millions of you who have had the courage to try something new. Now, I don't claim to be an expert on the British Constitution; but I forecast that sometime in the next 24 hours a message will come from the Palace asking me to appear before His Majesty. That would be the normal course for a situation where no one party has a majority. The party with the most seats, us The Angels, would normally be accorded first chance to form a Government.

If we are offered that chance then I shall propose a minority Government consisting solely of Angel MPs. We will invite a small number of existing politicians to leave their party allegiance

– decent people from across the political spectrum who have obtained a seat but on the ticket of another party. There are just a few such people, in my opinion, who can cast off 'politics as usual' and whose talents and opinions would be of real value to the whole community. But, even if they all came, we would be way short of a majority.

If invited by the King nevertheless to proceed, we will then put policies to Parliament. On the basis that, if we are voted down on anything that we consider vital, we will immediately resign and prepare for another Election. The Angels are ready and, in contrast to the bedraggled existing parties, financially able to do this. And, next time there is an Election, we will run candidates in every constituency in the UK. From the electorate's actions yesterday, I don't doubt that this second Election will secure us a majority.

Now I'll take questions but there really isn't much more I can or will say at this point. We will stand alone in Government or not at all."

Andrew listened to this short speech in silence. Of course, he realised, this was how Michael would play things; and with the great advantage that only the Angels had both the financial will and the personal beliefs to make a success of it. No messy or tawdry deals. Knowing Michael as Andrew now felt he did, the man would almost certainly have some early 'vital' policies ready to unleash next week that would appeal to voters and which would be difficult, if not impossible, for the other parties to vote down.

Andrew thought back to the turbulent 14 months since he had agreed to the Colonel's original plan. What had he got in that time? A girl whom he would follow to the ends of the Earth. A political platform in which he had faith. That was more than enough for him. And now, millions of voters had said they too wanted a future with real hope. They must not be denied.